JESSICA MARIN

To Tracey - thank you for your continued support, love, and encouragement. I owe you a lifetime of cheese curds and chocolate chip cookies.

Shopping FOR LOVE

Chapter One

ARI

A SLOW SMILE spreads across my face as I feel the warm breeze brush strands of my hair against my cheeks. I close my eyes and soak in the whimsical sounds of seagulls singing as they fly over the crashing waves against the shoreline. My sigh of contentment is for the sexy-as-sin Rodrigo as he appears, a drink in hand and a tantalizing smile transforming his lush full lips. Returning what I hope is a sexy smile back, my gaze slowly cascades down his rock-hard abs to his perfectly defined V, which disappears into his tropical boardshorts.

"This is heaven," I sigh, reaching out to grab my frozen piña colada.

"Watch out, lady!" he snarls, his whole demeanor changing unexpectedly.

"Watch what?" I question in confusion, not understanding what he's referring to or why his voice doesn't seem to match his looks.

With a flick of his wrist, Rodrigo sends the contents of my drink flying through the air. I watch it all happen in slow motion—specks of it landing on my face while the majority of it spills onto my chest and lap. I scream from the shock of coldness, and my hands immediately move to my eyes to rub the wet content out. As soon as they're clear, I open them slowly and again scream in dismay.

The clear, sunny sky was replaced with overcast, ugly clouds and freezing temperatures.

The white noise of seagulls and crashing waves were traded with blaring car horns.

My deserted beach was swapped with the dirty, busy intersection of Michigan Avenue and East Huron Street.

The piña colada, which I would have gladly let Rodrigo lick off my bare skin, was switched by dirty street water that's pooling at the street corner and is now soaking my fully clothed body.

To make matters even worse, the sexy, handsome Rodrigo was substituted with an older, overweight man yelling at me through the window of his vehicle with such force that spit spews out of his mouth.

"Lady, I almost made you roadkill!"

From the size of his truck, he's not exaggerating.

"Yeah, well… *you* need to watch out for pedestrians!" I yell back at him, my heart pounding with the same surge of adrenaline as if I just ran a marathon. I glance up at the pedestrian crossing to see the flashing orange hand, warning me not to step off curb and cross the street.

Damnit, I was in the wrong. I refuse to admit this to him. Why couldn't he see the ridiculous, goofy smile and glazed expression on my face? Clearly, I wasn't living in the moment of this harsh environment and was having one of the best daydreams of my life. I mean, no one who experiences winter in Chicago would be smiling like I was, if their mind was coherent.

I dared to look back at my newfound enemy, who revs ups his already loud engine and shakes his head at me.

"Get your head out of the clouds, lady," he shouts, and with a flash of his middle finger, drives away.

This isn't the first time my daydreaming has gotten me into

trouble, but this might be the closest I've come to death because of it. I've always been a daydreamer, but it seems to intensify during the winter months. I chalk it up to the obvious—I was not made for winter. Doesn't matter that I've lived my whole life here. My body despises winter. I'm the biggest, whiniest baby starting at Halloween and continuing to Easter. I can't stand when the cold permeates through my skin and muscles, making my bones shake and teeth rattle. I'm totally that friend who is perpetually cold and busts out the sweater onesies as soon as it drops below sixty degrees in the fall.

"Great, just great," I moan, inspecting my drenched clothes. I chose my coat for its warmth and style, not caring if it was water resistant or not. My sneakers and panty hose are waterlogged, and I figure I have less than a minute before the water soaking through my coat reaches my clothes and freezes me to death.

"I hate you winter," I growl, looking up at the sky and shaking my fist at it. I proceed to walk as fast as my now squeaking shoes can take me. My mood sours more when I realize I have to bypass buying my favorite morning coffee and scone in order to get to work early to try to dry off and make myself presentable. Fortunately, I have my work heels in my backpack with a make-up bag for emergencies like this.

The doors to the high-end department store I work for loom before me, and I take a deep breath, bracing myself for the stares and whispers that are about to ensue due to my appearance. Not that I care; the bitches who work here have always disliked me, but I don't lose any sleep over it.

Chin up, Ari! Your day is going to get better.

I nod at myself and walk in. With my shoulders back and head held high, I don't make eye contact with anyone while walking through the store and up the escalators to the second floor where my office is. As soon as I make it to my desk, I put my purse inside the bottom desk drawer and breathe out a sigh of relief.

"Jesus Christ, what the hell happened to you? You look like a lost, wet poodle."

I look over at my desk to where my only friend in this place sits and smirk at her, saying, "Thanks for not thinking of my feelings and sugar-coating anything."

"Since when do I ever sugar-coat anything? You love me *because* I tell it like it is. So spill the beans," Olivia demands, making her way toward my desk. She perches her hip against it, folds her arms across her chest, and raises one of her perfectly micro-bladed eyebrows at me.

"I don't want to talk about it," I grumble, giving her my best warning look, hoping in vain she stops asking.

"Yes, you do."

"No, I really don't."

"Why not? I'm concerned. You look like shit and I need to know what happened to try to help you fix it."

I roll my eyes at her, knowing full well she isn't *that* concerned.

"I got splashed with water. No big deal."

She looks me up and down before settling back on my face, her eyes narrowing. "You were daydreaming again, weren't you?"

"No, I wasn't," I declare quickly, my tone an octave above normal.

"Liar. How was Rodrigo this time?" she asks with a wicked glint in her eyes.

I should've never told her about Rodrigo. In my defense, I was trying to cheer her up when her boyfriend dumped her a couple of months ago. Nothing was working, even the three margaritas we consumed, so I told her. She laughed so hard she actually peed her pants.

"Whatever," I mumble and turn around, unable to meet her eyes. I'm not in the mood for a lecture. I decide to focus on myself instead and take off my coat to assess the damage underneath. I hang it up on the coat rack and look down at myself. My emerald-green, silk shirt is soaked and clinging to my chest, highlighting the outline of my lace bra. I rack my brain, trying to remember if I have any clients coming in today. Although even if I don't, I still don't want my co-workers to see me. The bitches of Bentley's will never let me live this one down.

"How bad is it?" Olivia asks, her footsteps stopping behind me.

I plaster a smile on my face and turn around.

"Not that bad," I say, lying to myself and her. "I don't have clients until this afternoon so I'm sure it will be dry by then."

"Ari, are you going blind? Honey, you're wearing silk and that beautiful water stain is already forming by your glorious tetas."

I can't help the snort that escapes my mouth at her calling my breasts their name in Spanish. Damnit, she's right and I nod reluctantly in agreement. The stain is totally going to be noticeable when it dries.

"Liv, I can't afford to buy anything new," I groan, wishing I had the kind of bank account that would allow me to shop here. But even with my seventy-five percent discount, I still can't pay for most things in this store. Maybe a pair of socks, and even then, that's pushing my budget.

"You're not going to be buying anything new. We're just going to borrow something for today." She winks at me with an evil grin. "Borrowing" means we either wear something with the tags on and return it, or take the tags off, dry clean it within twenty-four hours, and conveniently put the tags back on with our handy-dandy tagging gun. Employees do it all the time, but I haven't because it feels dishonest and wrong.

"No, no, no," I tell her with a firm shake of my head. "Olivia, I can't do that. You know with my luck I'll spill a whole bottle of foundation or something else on myself."

"We've got to do something, Ari. You can't look like this when Mr. Bentley comes in."

"Wait, *what*?" I freeze, praying to God I just didn't hear her correctly. "Mr. Bentley is coming in today?"

She confirms by nodding, and my stomach suddenly drops at a thought. "Which Mr. Bentley is coming?"

"The Mr. I-destroy-panties-with-one-smoldering-look Bentley."

"*No*," I gasp, my eyes widening in horror. The Bentley's have owned Bentley's of Chicago for eighty years and their grandson, Warren Bentley, is the current CEO of Bentley Corporations.

A young, deliciously *hot* CEO.

The notorious, bachelor-on-every-gossip-page-of-Chicago's finest tabloids CEO.

This can't be happening to me today. *Warren Bentley is coming into the store?*

"Mr. Bentley's assistant called right before you came in. He's personally coming in to pick up a present for his grandmother," Olivia mentions. I just stare at her, dumbfounded.

Not only is he technically my boss, but I'm also his designated shopper when he comes into the store, which hasn't happened in the four years I've been employed here. His assistant places his orders and either they come pick them up or we deliver the items to his office. This arrangement was enjoyable thus far because I know without a doubt, I would act like a bumbling idiot in front of him. He's *that* good-looking.

No man should be that good-looking.

"What time is he coming?" I breathe out in a shaky voice. With this news, I'm definitely going against my better judgement and borrowing something from the store. As soon as he leaves, I will return what I used. Easy-peasy. I got this.

Olivia looks at her watch and then grimaces. "He'll be here in fifteen minutes."

Shit!

The hysteria about to explode out of me must be apparent on my face because in one swift motion, Olivia grabs me by my biceps and shakes me, hard.

"I have a curling iron in my drawer. Grab it and your makeup bag and go to the restroom to fix your face. While you're doing that, I will find you a new dress to wear." She drops my arms and stands back while I continue to stare at her, frozen in fear. She snaps her fingers in my face, and I blink from the surprise of it. "Move that pretty ass of yours, Ari! We can do this!"

She runs out of the room and I quickly spring into action, raiding her desk for her curling iron. As I grab my stuff and race to the bathroom, I silently pray that we can pull this off and I don't get fired from a job I so desperately need.

Chapter Two

ARI

AN HOUR LATER, my nervousness is replaced by frustration. I've been standing by the main entrance of the store, feeling like a high-class hooker with the outfit Olivia picked out for me, and Mr. Bentley hasn't shown up yet. My feet are on fire from standing in these ridiculously tall, open-toe, high-heeled shoes I can barely walk in. I didn't have time to really look at myself in a full-length mirror before coming out here, and judging by the stares and whispers from my co-workers, I'm seriously questioning Olivia's sanity for picking out this dress.

"Ari, Olivia called and said you're needed at register six," my co-worker, Tempest, tells me while giving me a derisive once-over before walking away. I roll my eyes at her retreating back and decide to leave my post, not caring if Mr. Bentley comes in and I'm not there. I'm sure Tempest or any one of Bentley's bitch parade would jump at the chance to help him, and quite frankly, they can have at him. Days like today make me question my sanity for working here, but with the situation I'm in, I don't have a choice.

Slowly walking to register six, I make sure not to fall and make an even bigger ass of myself. Because my head was in the clouds again, I completely miss seeing Olivia racing toward me.

"He's here," she warns, grabbing my bicep and dragging me along. I flay my arms to regain my balance, causing Olivia to look back at me. "What's wrong with you? Stop walking like you're ninety!"

"These shoes are what's wrong with me," I hiss at her. "And what do you mean, he's here? His assistant told me he would be using the entrance off of Huron." I grit my teeth at the pain shooting through my feet due to our increased pace, mentally cursing both Olivia and Mr. Bentley.

"He came off of Michigan Avenue and proceeded to shop by himself before finally telling someone that he was here to meet you." She slows us down and stops ten feet away from the register. I see the backside of a tall man in a fine tailored suit and gulp down my anxiety. Olivia turns to stand in front of me, blocking my view, and grabs a hold of my hands. "Just warning you—he's even more scrumdiddlyumptious in person."

I shoot her a death glare while she walks away from me, laughing. I close my eyes and take a deep breath. *Breathe, Ari. Everything will be just fine.* I lift my chin, square my shoulders, and walk toward him with as much confidence that I can fake.

"Good morning, Mr. Bentley. I apologize for keeping you waiting." I announce my arrival as I walk around the glass countertop and stop dead in my tracks. I bite the insides of my cheek to keep my smile plastered on my face as piercing, blue eyes shoot daggers of annoyance at me. Even though Olivia warned me, my body was not prepared for the vision that is Warren Bentley. The man looks like he just stepped off a photo shoot for the latest Tom Ford Men's Suit collection. In the 2.5 seconds I've been in his presence, the air permeates with his confidence and delicious cologne, which is the perfect combination of musk and man. God, I want to bathe myself in his scent, but refrain from taking a deep whiff and moaning at how sensuous he smells. The man oozes sexiness, and all I want to do it lick and suck him up like a candy cane.

A candy cane? Seriously, Ari? You don't even like candy canes! I don't know what comes over me. I hide my hands behind the counter and grip the bottom of the display case, the pinching pain a welcome reminder to keep myself together and act professional. Looking up, I finally notice the scowl forming on his beautiful mouth.

"Why are all you ladies covering for Ari Leighton? Is it because he's not in the goddamn building? I'm getting fucking tired of this run-around with all of you trying to cover his ass. He's got some major balls making *me* wait for him."

And just like that, the raging flames of desire gripping my core are doused by his words. *What the hell?* He doesn't know that his personal shopper is a woman?

Asshole.

I clear my throat and mentally tell myself that this is my boss, and I can't call him every curse word rushing to my mind right now. "I'm Ari Leighton and if you would've come through the entrance your assistant told me you were going to use, you wouldn't have been waiting at all." I give him a cold smile and start to feel immensely satisfied watching his whole demeanor change from anger to shock. His gaze travels down to my nametag and he blinks a couple of times while staring at it, as if trying to decipher what it says. "Ari is short for Ariana, and I've been waiting for you for an hour at the Huron Street entrance of the store."

I notice the muscle in his jaw tick while his glance moves from my nametag to flicker over the V-neck of my dress before traveling up my collar and face to look me in the eyes. I feel the heat of a blush tainting my cheeks from the intensity of his stare, which unnerves me.

"Why don't you go by Ariana?" he rudely asks, surprising me with his question. *Why is that any of his business?*

"Because it sounds pretentious, which is the complete opposite of who I am." I can't help my condescending tone, nor can I stop myself from giving him a piece of his own medicine. I deliberately rake my eyes slowly up and down his fine, sculpted body, knowing full well his gaze is on me.

His lips twitch in amusement.

"Well, that's good to know," he responds before clearing his throat. "Let's get down to business." He brings forth the items on his right for me to inspect. "While I was waiting, I picked out some items that I think might be appropriate for my grandmother's Christmas gift. She leaves soon for an extended trip to Australia and New Zealand, so we'll be exchanging gifts early. I would like to hear your opinion on them."

That's it? No apology for his rudeness, for making *me* wait, or for assuming I was a man? Disappointment rears its ugly head at knowing that he's just another rich douchebag who's used to getting his way due to his money and power.

I shake off my disgust and nod my acknowledgement at his request, grateful to move on to the reason he's here, and hopefully, get him out of here quickly. The first item he chose is the latest Judith Leiber purse, and I mentally question why when he bought her one exactly like it three months ago for her birthday. I know this because *I* picked it out for him. The next item is an ugly ruby and emerald tiger broach. Doesn't matter if the gems are real, it is Fugly with a capital F.

Ugh, he gets her a broach every year and I have never seen her wear any of them when she comes into the store or in pictures of her in magazines.

I keep my poker face on for the very last gift, an Etro embroidered cape in colors that are so bright, it looks like a child colored all over it.

"I'm assuming you're shopping for Mrs. Bentley?" I ask, even though I already know the answer since he has only one remaining grandmother. Christine Bentley is sophisticated, classy, and a timeless beauty even in her seventies. Bentley's of Chicago was her baby, and her vision was for it to be North America's version of Harrod's of London. Once Bentley's of Chicago reached that status, she let her son-in-law take charge and retired with her husband to travel the world. Since the death of the elder Mr. Bentley, she rarely comes in anymore, but when she does, I always admire her grace and kindness as she stops to greet every employee in the building.

"Yes, it's for her. Do you know my grandmother?" he inquires with a raised eyebrow.

"Not personally, but she's always gracious whenever she comes in," I answer honestly. From what I have observed of Mrs. Bentley, none of these items seem to be her style, which makes me wonder how close Warren and his grandmother really are.

"Any woman would be ecstatic to receive these luxurious items, but I had something else in mind for your grandmother that I would like to show you. If that's okay?" I ask, not wanting him to think I would know what's better for his grandmother than he would.

"Are you implying what I picked out isn't suitable?" That damn eyebrow raises again, and I would love nothing more than to douse his haughtiness with a nice cup of ice-cold water.

"Not at all. Since it's my job to shop for you and upon request, members of your family, I thought presenting you with a couple more ideas would be helpful. If your mind is made up on these items, then by all means, don't let me waste your time by showing you other options."

The sexy smirk he bestows on me only fuels my annoyance with him. *Stop thinking he's sexy, Ari. He's a jerk!*

"By all means, please show me what you had in mind," he purrs.

My nod is curt as I turn and walk away from him. When he's out of earshot, I sigh, letting out an exhausted breath and hoping this day goes by quickly; it's been a doozie and it's only ten-thirty in the morning. It takes me only five minutes to retrieve what I need and rejoin him at the register.

"Since you mentioned she will be traveling, I picked out gifts that might be more suitable for her trip. This stylish zipped bag contains the perfect travel accessories of a satin lined eye mask, a down alternative travel pillow, and this beautiful, gray throw blanket she can use when it gets cold on the airplane." I pull out the contents of the bag and he inspects each item thoroughly. I watch him rub the blanket between his finger pads, making me wonder if they're calloused or smooth. But then I remember who he is and the world he grew up in. His fingers are probably as smooth as a baby's butt. Callouses would require him to do manual labor and I doubt this man has done anything physical in his life besides lifting weights and having sex. Also, why am I getting flushed at the thought of his fingertips? *No, Ari, don't you dare go there.*

"The next item I want to show you is this envelope travel organizer from Abas. It is made from this magnificent full-quill ostrich from South Africa and can easily hold her passport, currency, and any other cards she needs to carry. This fits perfectly in her carry-on or any other medium sized bag she might use while being a tourist down under."

I ignore another one of his smirks and focus on the last item on my list. This one is my favorite and I feel a little sad showing it to him. Not that I could afford to buy it for myself, but there's just something majestic about this floral scarf that I love. It's made of the finest of silks Italy has to offer and the painting of pastel flowers transports you to an enchanted garden. I don't even care for floral prints, but this gorgeous scarf seems special and makes me sigh with happiness. But I could never afford a scarf like this.

"Since it's summertime in the Southern Hemisphere, I thought this scarf would be perfect for Mrs. Bentley. It's light enough to wear during the day and fancy enough for evenings out. The colors of this scarf go perfectly with her skin tone and would accentuate her blue eyes."

Warren's head snaps up from the scarf and he stares at me, a weird expression crossing over his face. Unable to stand his scrutiny, I start folding the scarf back up and shift uncomfortably on my feet. I clear my throat and decide to break the silence.

"Whatever you decide to choose for her, I can take to get gift-wrapped."

That seems to break him out of whatever trance he's in. He looks back down and studies everything once more before making his decision.

"I'll take everything you suggested," he says, making me want to yell out in victory. "And add the broach to it." He grabs the small box and puts it next to my pile.

I quickly gather everything up and nod at him.

"I'll be right back," I announce and proceed to go to the gift-wrapping room. There are no customers in here yet, so one of the ladies helps me wrap up his gifts. We work fast, but meticulously, especially since we know who everything is going to. We're done in under fifteen minutes and I bag them all up in one of our branded tote bags with tissue paper.

"I hope Mrs. Bentley loves everything you picked out for her," I tell him when I return. I hand over the bag and jump from the unexpected jolt of electricity when his fingers graze over mine.

"Right, well, um," he stutters while looking around uncomfortably. He glances at his Rolex, refusing to look me in the eyes. "Thanks for your help and it's a pleasure meeting you." With a curt nod, he walks past me to leave.

I turn around to watch him exit the building, my head shaking in disbelief at what just transpired.

"Wish I could say the same," I mutter, praying this is the only time I ever have to deal with Warren Bentley in person again.

Chapter Three

WARREN

"WHAT THE FUCK was that, Warren?" I ask myself in disgust as soon as my driver shuts the car door. I just acted like a complete shithead for no reason except that I wasn't prepared for Ariana Leighton to knock me off my game.

The first shock was her not being a man like I assumed her to be from her name. This just goes to show you that you should never assume a person's gender by their name. I presumed she was a man because every Ari I've known or heard of *was* a man. Instead, she's a naturally stunning beauty who would turn heads anywhere she went. Usually I'm calm, cool, and collected when meeting gorgeous women like Ari, but I'm not usually taken by surprise. Meeting her was like receiving a surprise gift—not expecting it at all but liking it.

The second shock was her sharp tongue and sassiness. No one has ever stood up to me the way she did. She rendered me speechless, and yet throughout our whole exchange, all I kept fantasizing about was shutting her up by claiming her luscious mouth. She was unimpressed by who I was, my faux pas at assuming she was a male only making her disdain me more. Most women would have laughed my mistake off in order to hold my attention, but Ariana made it clear she didn't give a rat's ass who I was and was completely insulted by my assumption. The memory of the sexy, petite spitfire with her sparkling hazel eyes shooting daggers at me makes my dick twitch.

Calm down, asshole. We're her boss. She's off-limits.

I've never entertained the idea of dating an employee before. I was warned at a young age to never *ever* dip my stick in that type of candy, no matter how tempting it may be. There are plenty of beautiful women who work for Bentley Corporation and not one of them were hired for their looks. If they're smart *and* good-looking, that's just an added bonus. We do have it in our HR manual that we prefer employees to not fraternize outside of the office, but I've seen how crazy our holiday parties get with the open bar we provide. I know people are fucking outside office hours.

Still, not one employee has affected me the way Ariana has—hell, no woman for that matter. I've never felt bad about being an asshole before to someone, but she didn't deserve my behavior and quite honestly, I don't like how that makes me feel. The urge to go back into the store and apologize is strong, but I was so deep into my thoughts that I didn't realize my driver had already taken off.

How has that beauty been my personal shopper for four years and I'm now just discovering her?

I reach into my coat pocket to retrieve my cell phone and call my sister, Delilah, who also happens to be my assistant. "Hey, I'm on my way into the office," I tell her when she picks up her phone.

"Good, because we have a lot of things to tackle on your schedule today before you go see grandmother. Did you grab her gift?"

"I did and speaking about that, did you know my personal shopper was a woman?"

"Yeah, so what?"

"It would've been nice if I was told that," I growl at her in frustration. "This whole time I thought she was a man and I just made an ass out of myself."

"That's a daily occurrence for you," she responds sarcastically, the clicking of her keyboard while she types carrying through the phone. "Why should this time bother you compared to the other times?"

"I don't purposely try to be a jerk to people, Delilah. You should have prepared me better. Besides, how many women do you know go by the name 'Ari'? I only know men with that name."

"It's not my problem you only know men named Ari. Furthermore, you're being a little prick right now because you know damn well it isn't my fault you don't take the time to look at people's emails. If you did, you would've seen that her email address states her name as Ariana Leighton."

"You're the one who handles orders to the store, so why would I bother reading those emails when I know you're handling it?"

"Because that's what CEOs do. They read every email that deals with their business."

"Well then what's the point of you? Guess I need to terminate your position," I tease because we both know that would never happen in a million years. Delilah wanted no part of the family business and it took a lot of begging and an exuberant amount of money to get her to agree to be my executive assistant. Once my father handed over the reins to me, it was imperative that I had an assistant who I could trust. Delilah and my grandmother are the only people on that list.

"Can we just agree that you'll start paying better attention to your emails and who they come from, even if they're subjects I normally handle?"

"I'll try my best." I chuckle at her groan of annoyance. Annoying my sister never gets old, even as an adult. "I didn't get a chance to apologize though. Maybe I should send her flowers?"

"What? That's a horrible idea. We would be out of business if we sent apology flowers to every woman you were rude to."

"You're so dramatic. Seriously, it's the right thing to do."

"Seriously, it's not. Who are you and what have you done

with my brother?"

"Delilah—"

"No, you listen to me, Warren. I've met Ari in person before so I know *exactly* how beautiful she is. Whatever ideas you are entertaining about trying to see her again need to end. She's an employee and you will leave her alone."

"The whole city of Chicago and I hear you loud and clear. I'm pulling up to the office. See you in a few." I end the call before giving her a chance to respond.

The car stops in front of our office building and I exit the car without waiting for my driver to open the door. I inhale the crisp air and try to make a decision about what I want to do regarding an apology to Ari. Flowers are a bad idea because it will lead to unnecessary gossip. Emails are too impersonal. The only other option would be in-person. I can't contain my smile at the thought of seeing Ari again at the store—this time a surprise visit would need to be in order so Delilah doesn't see it on my schedule and yell at me. Afterall, I will need to buy Delilah a Christmas gift without her knowing.

I know the consequences of dating one of my employees, but leaving Ariana Leighton alone is the last thing I want to do. Delilah just doesn't need to know about it.

I LEAVE MY office at a quarter to five to meet my grandmother for dinner at her house. The ride is short since she recently moved to a penthouse in the city with a spectacular view of Lake Michigan. Once the car pulls up to her building, I grab the gift bag and exit the vehicle, nodding to the doorman as he greets me while opening the door for me. I follow the hallway to the private elevators that only go up to the penthouses and get in.

"My boy," my grandmother says in greeting once she opens her door. I give her a kiss on the cheek and walk in.

"You look beautiful as always, grandmother." Christine Bentley takes care of herself with daily exercises and meditation. Despite being in her seventies, she doesn't look a day older than sixty with her colored hair and almost wrinkle-free skin thanks to Botox and fillers.

"Why, thank you, Warren. Had to dress up for my hot date tonight," she teases with a wink. She's wearing one of her vintage tweed Chanel suites with low-heeled shoes. Her blonde hair is tied up in her signature chignon and her make-up is perfectly in place. "You look like your usual devilishly handsome self in that suit. Have you been behaving yourself lately?"

"Of course not. When have you known me to behave?"

She slowly shakes her head, a smile playing on her lips. "I feel bad for all of the women whose hearts break just by looking at you." I grin at her joke and follow her to the living room. "Let's sit down and have a pre-dinner cocktail, shall we?"

"Are we going out for dinner or staying in?" I inquire while heading to the wet bar to make us a drink.

"Staying in. I want to get to bed early tonight since I have a busy day with my long flight. I had the chef prepare one of your favorite, brisket with potatoes and broccoli."

I nod my approval at her and carry our drinks over to where she is sitting down. "What do you plan on doing before your flight tomorrow?"

"Just tie up some loose ends since I'll be gone for over a month and I plan visiting with an old friend."

"Well, here's to you, Grandmother." I lift up my drink for a toast to her. "I hope you have safe travels and that you meet some hunky Australian to bring in the New Year with."

"Your words to God's ears, my boy." She laughs and clinking her glass with mine before taking a sip of our drinks. My grandmother is all talk when it comes to meeting someone. My grandfather died five years ago and she hasn't made any efforts to find companionship. She travels the world by herself, telling us she refuses to sit at home and let her soul die while there's so much to see in her little time left on Earth. I hate that she's alone, but she claims our grandfather was the love of her life and she's content at being alone until the time comes for her to see him again on the other side.

"Are you ready for your Christmas gift, grandmother?"

"Warren, I told you before that I wish you would stop buying me gifts," she scolds, pointing her manicured index finger at me. "You coming over for dinner and spending time with me is all I'll ever want."

"Just say thank you and open your gifts," I demand because we both know I'm not going to stop buying her presents. She rolls her eyes and takes the bag from me.

"At least you have remarkable taste and shop at my favorite store." Her eyes light up as she grabs the first present out of the bag. This is my favorite part. The woman has everything you could ever want but seeing her happiness at receiving items from her own store is priceless.

"I thought I would be disowned if I shopped somewhere else," I tease and it's probably somewhat true.

"Fired and disowned," she says seriously, making me chuckle.

She unwraps the small box, opens it and starts to laugh. "This, my dear boy, is hideous and probably the best one you've picked out so far. When are the gag gifts of broaches going to end? You know I won't wear them."

"Don't worry, I'll sell them all when you die," I tell her with a wicked grin. "Better yet, I think you should leave them in your will for Delilah and nothing else. She'll be so pissed."

She giggles at the idea because she knows Delilah would be beyond herself if she was left with them. "Evil, but I actually think the part of leaving them to her is brilliant."

She puts the broach down and grabs another gift out of the bag to unwrap. "This is pretty," she exclaims when she opens the box. She takes the envelope organizer out and opens it. "Oh, it's one of those travel wallets that fits your passport, cash and cards. This is a great gift for my trip!" She looks surprised as she rubs her fingers across the material.

"That's full-quail ostrich from South Africa you're stroking," I inform her, impressed with myself for even remembering that tidbit from Ari. My grandmother's head snaps up and her nose wrinkles in disgust. "Oh c'mon now. Let's not be a hypocrite. You have a whole closet full of dead cows in the form of purses and shoes." She hits me in the arm with her gift, causing me to laugh because she knows I'm right.

"I don't need to be reminded of what they're made of. In fact, I declare right now that you're not allowed to buy me anything made with real leather or any other kind of material that was made from an animal." She pulls out the next present, which happens to be the bag containing the eye-mask and blanket. "Like this bag is perfect and made from high-quality material other than an animal."

"So are you suggesting I take back the ostrich travel organizer?"

"I didn't suggest anything of the sort," she responds with a straight face.

"That's what I thought," I answer with a smirk.

She's opening her last present and I focus my gaze on her face, curious to watch her expression when she sees the scarf. "Oh my word, Warren," she exclaims in shock. "This is stunning!" She unfolds the scarf and wraps it around her neck, fingering the fabric while she inspects the design of the flowers. Ari was right, her blue eyes look brighter and the colors of the scarf go well with her skin.

"My boy, you've outdone yourself this time with these gifts." She pulls the scarf off her neck and gazes at it in admiration. "They are perfect and I will actually get to use them on my trip." She studies me closely before concentrating on folding the scarf backup. "Your shopper did an amazing job."

"Why do you think it was my shopper this time around and not me?" I place my hand over my heart to pretend to be insulted.

"Too much attention to detail, my boy. That area is not your forte." I chuckle at her accuracy and how well she knows me.

"You're right, but I did actually go into the store this time to approve them rather than over photos in an email." Images of Ariana start to cloud my vision, making me wonder if my grandmother knows who she is. One of my grandmother's best qualities is remembering every name and face of the employees who worked for her. "Grandmother, do you remember my shopper Ari Leighton?"

Her eyes light up at the name. "I do remember Ariana. I

know her mother better though because she was one of our store managers."

"She was?" I rack my brain to recall her name, but come up empty. The store used to fall under my father's care, but since he's living a new life with his much younger wife, I've been involved more with it, taking meetings with the Chief Operation Officer and General Manager of the store.

"Angela Leighton is her mother." She goes quiet for a moment, the emotions on her face turning to sadness. "You know, even though you and Ariana come from different worlds, you do have another thing in common besides the store." She looks down at her hands before continuing. "Her mother is dying of ovarian cancer."

I inhale sharply, not expecting to hear that. "What stage?" I question gruffly, my voice going hoarse from the unexpected emotions that the word cancer brings out of me. Even though it has been fifteen years since my mother succumbed to her battle with ovarian cancer, it still feels like yesterday when I held her hand as she took her last breath.

"Stage 4." Her eyes tear up and I reach for her hand to give it a reassuring squeeze. "It's the reason why Ariana came to work for us actually."

"What do you mean?"

"Ariana was in her third year of law school at Northwestern when her mother got diagnosed. I'll never forget the day Angela was screaming with excitement throughout the store when Ariana got accepted and was awarded a full scholarship." She smiles at the memory before shaking her head to clear it away. "Anyway, Ariana dropped out to help her parents. Ariana's father owns his own construction firm. It's very small and he's very hands on, so he's always busy. Ariana helped out by taking her mother to all of her medical appointments and sitting with her while she did chemotherapy. But when Angela became too weak to work, they needed another income fast to help pay for her medical bills. That's when Ariana came to work for Bentley's."

"So if she was going to law school, was she working on the side as a personal shopper?" My grandmother's cheeks turn red and she refuses to look me in the eye, the answer written all over her face. "You hired her with no experience in order to help them out, didn't you?"

"Angela became a dear friend when your grandfather passed and as much as I love her, she's too stubborn for her own good. I tried to help out, but she would rip up every check I would give her. So the next best thing I could think of to help was to hire Ariana. Fortunately, Ariana has natural style and is smart, so she eased into the role without any problems."

I slowly digest this information about Ariana, the pieces of the puzzle starting to fit together. A full scholarship to Northwestern confirms her intelligence. With her mother so sick, her job is to help contribute to the bills. She unselfishly gave up her dreams to help her family. It seems that not only is she beautiful on the outside, but has a beautiful soul on the inside as well.

I snap out of my fog and lean in to give my grandmother a kiss on her cheek. "You're an amazing woman, Christine Bentley."

She shakes her head and waves off my words. "No, I'm not. We both know what it's like to watch someone we love dying of cancer and I hate it for Angela, but more so for Ariana to have to go through this alone. She has no siblings and her father throws himself into his work, his denial has apparently overtaken him."

I can't deny that watching my mother die didn't harden me, but I have no idea what type of person I would've become if it wasn't for Delilah and my grandparents. My father has been devoid of emotion for as long as I can remember, so it was my sister and grandparents who were there for me.

"Please don't let Ariana know what I told you. The Leighton's are very private people and she would be mortified if she knew that you know her home life situation or how she came to Bentley's. She doesn't even know that her mother and I are friends." She grabs my forearm and looks at me with pleading eyes. "Please Warren, don't say anything to her and for heaven's sake, please don't be rude to her."

Too late for that.

"Your secrets are safe with me, grandmother. Delilah is the one that usually places orders with Ari and I promise I won't say a word to her." I pat my grandmother's hand and decide to change the subject, even though my mind is demanding to ask more questions. "I'm starving. Let's go enjoy that delicious meal your chef made for us."

I offer my hand to help her out of her chair and escort her to the dining room. Even though the discussion about Ariana is now over, thoughts of her and how I plan to insert myself into her life start to form.

CHRISTINE BENTLEY

As SOON AS my grandson leaves for the night, I retrieve my cell phone and call the one person who I've been dying to talk to.

"Angie, are you alone?" I ask once she picks up the phone.

"Chris? Is everything all right?" Despite her concern, she sounds worn-out and my heart breaks at what she's going through.

"Yes, are you alone?" I repeat, not wanting to continue the conversation if her family was around.

"Yes, I'm alone. Tom is working and Ariana is getting us food. The poor thing burnt dinner again," she sighs with worry. "She was so upset. More so than usual for some reason. I told her it was no big deal and to go get takeout. Thankfully, she didn't argue with me and did it. She should be back soon, so we don't have very long to chat."

"It's happening, Angie!" I tell her with excitement, cutting right to the chase. "Fate is intervening."

"What do you mean?" she asks in confusion. "What about fate?"

"What is the one thing you and I always wished for together?" I ask and hear her gasp in surprise.

"They finally met?"

"Yes! He went into the store today and let me tell you, he's intrigued."

"No offense, Chris, but your boy seems to be intrigued by a lot of women," she says with a sarcastic laugh. "I can't have Ari getting hurt. She's been through so much already and it's only going to get worse."

My throat tightens and I squeeze my eyes close, not wanting to think of what's going to come next for Angie. "Like all men, he's just sowing his wild oats right now. I think once he meets the right woman, he'll be completely smitten and loyal."

"We don't know if Ari will be the one for him."

"Angie, I feel it in my bones. I feel this is meant to be."

"We'll see, Chris, but please don't get your hopes up. I don't want you to get disappointed." I'm about to chastise her for being so negative when she interrupts me before I get the chance. "Chris, she's home. I've got to go. I'll see you tomorrow," she whispers and hangs up on me.

I put down my phone and sigh. "Please Warren, prove me wrong. See that Ariana is meant for you," I pray out loud. "You're meant for each other."

And what that, I'll let fate do its part and not interfere.

Chapter Four

ARI

I MAKE MY way slowly down Michigan Avenue to work the next morning, my legs, body and mind exhausted from yesterday's activities. Warren Bentley occupied most of my thoughts well after he left. I'm so angry at myself for letting him take up so much of my mental time, but it's like my brain wants to keep torturing me with memories of how handsome he is. It shouldn't matter what he looks like. He was rude and therefore, should fall into the category of 'douchebags your brain should never conjure up again.' But no, *my* stupid brain wanted me to not only think about him after he left, but also on the train ride home, and while cooking dinner—which eventually caused me to burn dinner—and to top it off, I *dreamt* about him.

Not only should you never have a dream about your sexy, unattainable boss, but you should also never dream about having dirty, hot, angry sex with same said boss. The sex in my dream felt so real that I screamed out my orgasm, causing my father to rush into my room with a baseball bat because he thought I was being attacked.

Yup, mortifying. And I don't even like angry sex.

Wait, have I even had angry sex?

For me to even be questioning if I have or haven't leads me to think I have *not* because I would hope I would've remembered having sex the way I had it in my dream with Warren. Not that I have much experience in that department. I've only had sex with two different people and both were mediocre at best. My vibrators are collecting dust since I'm too mortified to use them under my parent's roof.

I shake my head at myself and how pathetic my life sounds. I'm a twenty-seven-year-old, law school dropout living at home with her parents. No boyfriend and barely any friends. Every time I start my pity party for one, I tell myself that none of that matters right now. What matters is every single second I have with my mom.

I'm not naive—I know her time is borrowed and the sand in her hourglass is almost up. She's a shell of her former self; a skeleton with sickly skin and eyes too bright for their own good. She's been battling hard against her cancer for four years, being told twice she was in remission only to have it rear its ugly head back with a vengeance. She has five more weeks of her latest chemotherapy treatment and it seems that this current round is kicking her ass. If her scans come back showing the cancer has continued to spread, then she's requested to stop all treatment.

Don't cry, Ari, not before work, I reprimand myself as I wipe a lone tear off my cheek. Olivia is the only person at work who knows my home life situation, and I've sworn her to secrecy to not breathe a word to anyone else. I'm not ready for the sympathetic stares or the "poor Ari" looks quite yet. As much as I loathe my co-workers, I do like the fact that my job distracts me from my reality. I get to make people feel happy with themselves or buying things for others.

My rumbling stomach breaks me from my thoughts, and I notice I'm almost at my favorite coffee shop. I remind myself to focus on my surroundings so that nothing stops me from having my coffee and scone like it did yesterday.

The line is small when I arrive and the fresh, delicious aroma of coffee brings a smile to my face. I bask in the warmth of the shop and its holiday decor while I wait. The line moves quickly and in no time, it's my turn to order.

"Good morning, Ari. Are you having your usual this morning?" Mrs. Johnston, the owner of the store, asks in her rich New Orleans accent.

"Yes, ma'am. Are you doing okay this morning?" I ask her while she yells out my order to one of her employees making the coffee.

"Blessed as usual, Ms. Ari. How about—" Her question dies on her lips, her eyes going wide and her mouth parting slightly as she gazes at something over my right shoulder.

"Mrs. Johnston? Are you all right?" But as soon as I ask my question, my pulse starts to unexpectedly race, the hairs on the back of my neck rise, and that's when I smell a familiar scent. One that seems to have engrained itself into my nostrils.

Warren.

"I'll be paying for her order," he commands while sliding up next to me, laying a fifty-dollar bill on the counter.

"No, you will not," I growl, slamming my credit card down as well, jolting Mrs. Johnston out of her Warren trance.

"Oh my, Ari. Is this handsome stud your boyfriend?" I watch her face transform into a googly-eyed, smiling piece of mush while she giggles shyly at Warren. I look over just in time to see him wink at her.

Ugh, is there anyone on this planet who's immune to his charm?

"No, he's the devil," I grumble in disgust. I hear his chuckle and I refuse to even look his way. I wave my credit card in front of her face, trying to regain her attention. "Please take my credit card and charge it."

She looks between us before leaning over her register, signaling for me to come closer to her. "Ari, when a man who looks like that wants to pay for you, you don't argue and accept with gratitude," she whispers at me, but loud enough for Warren to hear her words.

He slides his money closer to her, gives her a genuine smile, and says, "Keep the change."

And just like that, he won.

"Oh my, why thank you, sir. We appreciate your generosity." She bats her eyelashes at him, and I feel like I'm going to throw up. Her employee brings my order to her to give to me, but instead, Mrs. Johnston hands it to Warren. "You come back and see me again, sugar."

She watches Warren hand me the bag and coffee and giggles when she realizes her mistake. "Oops, sorry, Ari."

"Traitor." I mouth, angry at her for succumbing to his charm and good looks. I feel his strong hands on the small of my back as he urges me to step away from the counter so another customer can have their turn. My pulse races at his touch and I purposely walk faster to get away from him. The line has gotten longer and I manage to squeeze through the bodies gathering at the entrance and slip out.

"Ari, stop," he demands, and I hate myself a little because I obey.

I turn around and glare, not caring that we're in the middle of the sidewalk with people walking by us. "What are you doing here, Mr. Bentley?"

"I was on my way to the store when I saw you walking, so I followed you here. Also, please call me Warren."

"That's creepy. Guess I need to call HR on you, *Mr. Bentley*." My answer is rewarded with a smirk and already I can feel my traitorous body responding to him. The bastard knows nothing would even happen to him if I did call HR, which I wouldn't do anyway.

"I owe you an apology for my behavior yesterday and I wanted to do it in-person."

"An email would have sufficed," I tell him before turning on my heel to walk to work.

"No, that wouldn't have been appropriate," he says, easily catching up with me in two long strides.

"And following me *is* appropriate?" I shoot him an incredulous look at his rational.

"I didn't mean to follow you. I just happened to see you

while we were driving to the store." He's annoyed at my lack of understanding and I smile, internally enjoying his frustration.

"Fine, apology accepted. Now you can leave."

"I'm walking with you."

"Why? You don't need to go to the store anymore. Don't you have companies to divide and conquer?"

"It's my store, I don't need an excuse to stop by."

I stop in my tracks, catching him by surprise because he passes me by. I place my hands on my hips and glare at him when he turns around. We both know that's not his reason. Warren never comes to the store and takes all store related meetings at his office.

His eyes twinkle with wicked mischief, making me want to stomp my foot in irritation. "Nice to have your attention finally. Now, will you please listen to me?"

I grit my teeth and curtly nod at him. I don't want him to apologize because that means I have to forgive him. I also don't want to stare into those gorgeous aquamarine eyes of his. They remind me of the ocean and when I think of the ocean, images of Warren and I at a deserted beach start to form.

No daydreaming, Ari! Rodrigo is your daydreaming lover, not your boss!

"I'm sorry for not following my assistant's directions and making you wait at the wrong entrance for me. I'm also sorry I was a presumptuous prick at assuming you were a male. Clearly, you are far from being one." He purposely rakes his eyes up and down my body, and suddenly, I don't feel the frigid air anymore. His lips transform into a heart-stopping smile, causing my heart to flutter and my blood to warm. My eyes are drawn to his full lips like magnets, making me wonder what they taste like.

Stop looking at his lips, Ari.

Someone's cough brings me out of my Warren trance and I hear it again. It is one of those deep coughs that is sounds like it hurts from being settled deep in the lungs.

"Can we pretend yesterday didn't happen and start over?" I barely hear Warren's question as my attention zones in on where the cough is coming from. I step to my right to see a homeless man up ahead sitting on the ground against a building. He's huddled together to keep himself warm, but I can see his body shivering.

"Start over?" I softly repeat, but my mind is on the man ahead. I look down at the cup in my hand and sigh in resignation.

"Yes, start over. Like this." My eyes wander back to Warren as he holds out his hand for me to shake. "Hi, I'm Warren Bentley, CEO of Bentley Corporation and I'm asking you to accept my apology for being an asshole yesterday." A boyish smile tugs at his lips and he bats his long eyelashes at me. I close my eyes and groan, trying to regain my composure. God, he's good because already I can feel myself calming under his charm. I open my eyes back up to respond but nothing comes to mind. All I can think about is the homeless man.

I hold up my palm to indicate I need a minute. "Hold that thought, please." I walk around him and march straight to the homeless man ahead of me.

"Hear you go, sir. I hope you enjoy it." I hand him my coffee and scone before reaching into my purse and grabbing the only cash I have on me. "And here's five dollars. Sorry, that's all I have, but you need to promise me you won't buy drugs or alcohol with it." I hold it out of his reach, not giving it to him unless he promises.

"Lady, in what country do you know of where you can score drugs or alcohol for five dollars?"

"Huh." I ponder what he says while he looks at me as if I'm the stupidest person he's ever met.

"When you figure it out, let me know," he says, and I give in and hand him the bill. "Thanks for this, lady." He salutes me with the cup of coffee before taking a sip, a small smile forming on his lips.

"You're welcome," I respond, hoping it gives him some temporary warmth. I look away from him to see Warren standing next to me, staring at me intensely. I tilt my head in the direction of the store and we walk the remaining three blocks in comfortable silence. I can't tell what he's thinking, and quite frankly, I don't care if he's upset that I gave away the coffee and scone he bought me. I didn't ask him to do that and I would've still given it to the homeless man even if I paid for it. It was the right thing to do. I take a quick peak at him from the corner of my eye to see if his expression gives anything away. His mouth is turned into a frown, but he doesn't look angry. He looks as if he's having a serious internal discussion with himself.

Before we get to the employee entrance, I stop and decide that I need to act like the professional that I am. This man didn't have to apologize to me at all. He probably eats up and spits out employees every day at headquarters. It's time to let what happened yesterday go and just move on.

"Hi, I'm Ari Leighton, your personal shopper." I offer him my hand and I watch his large, gloved hand slowly encase mine in a firm grip. I gaze at our hands for a few seconds before looking back up at him. "You're forgiven... this time." I surprise myself and him by giving him a wink.

His chuckle is rich and deep, and I swear to sweet baby Jesus, I can feel it vibrating throughout my core.

Wow, Ari, you really are pathetic if this guy's laugh is making your panties wet.

"Thanks for accepting my apology... and not reporting me to HR," he jokes back, and any residual anger I may harbor toward him completely vanishes. I like joking, smiling Warren. He's fun and adorable. *And completely dangerous for my heart.*

"Well, thanks for walking me to work. Oh, and for the breakfast," I grin sheepishly at him.

"It was my pleasure," he says in a soothing, husky voice that captures my attention and once again, I focus on his lips and imagine what they would feel like.

He clears his throat, and my gaze snaps up to see he caught me staring at him. I feel myself turning as red as a tomato, my instincts telling me to get the hell out of there before I do anything else to embarrass myself.

"Welp, got to go," I announce hastily. "Send me an email if you need anything." I don't wait for his response as I turn around, grab the door handle and practically run inside.

Chapter Five

WARREN

I STARE AT the contract sitting in front of me, trying to focus on the same sentence I have re-read ten times already, but it's no use. My brain is fucked up and the cause of it is Ariana Leighton.

It's been two days since our encounter at the coffee shop and my mind won't stop replaying how she looked staring at my lips. If her eyes were laser beams, she would've burned them off with how much raw desire I saw in them. I've jerked off four times to the memory of that look and it only confirms what I know is going to happen. I want Ariana Leighton and nothing will stand in my way.

Not even the fact that she's one of my employees.

"Fuck," I groan and throw down my pen, giving up on the contract. No woman has consumed my thoughts the way she has. I feel like a crazed lunatic with how I feel about her and it's kind of scaring the crap out of me. Yes, I'm insanely attracted to her physically, but it's her unselfishness and caring for others that mesmerized me. Watching her give her breakfast and money to that homeless man was an eye-opening experience. Most women who run in my circles would've been scared to even walk by him, let alone talk to him. Her actions today combined with what my grandmother told me about her giving up her dreams for her family, proves that she's a diamond in the rough and I would be a damn fool to let her slip away.

Since Ariana is not like most woman, asking her out will prove to be challenging. I'm one hundred percent confident that she would turn me down if I asked her to dinner. Given the status of our professional relationship, I need to be strategic in how I plan on pursuing her, which annoys the shit out of me. The dominant male inside of me just wants to take control of her mind, body, and soul, but I know with her I'll have to tread lightly. A knock on my door interrupts my thoughts and without waiting for my response, my sister barrels into my office.

"You know, you really should wait for me to give you permission to enter. What if I was relieving myself from the stress of this job with an afternoon jerk-off?"

"Then I expect you to lock your door if you plan on being a disgusting pig." She starts to dry heave, her face scrunched up in disgust. "Ew, why did you have to scar me with that visual? You're my brother, for Pete's sake!"

She looks so ridiculous trying to shake out whatever image of me is in her head that I start to laugh uncontrollably. When her movements stop, I take a couple of deep breaths to calm down. "You really are the best, Delilah. Thanks for the laugh. I needed that."

"You're welcome, but I actually wasn't trying to be funny. Don't you even think for one second of entertaining the idea of pleasuring yourself inside this office. You hear me?"

"Do you really think I would ever do that?"

She stares at me for a few seconds before answering. "I guess not."

"Geez, thanks for sounding so reassuring."

"You're welcome. Can we please move on to the reason why I came in?"

"I thought you would never ask," I reply sarcastically, ignoring the death glare she gives me.

"I've been fielding phone calls regarding your attendance to numerous holiday parties that you've been invited to. Can you please go through these and make a yes and no pile?"

She throws down a huge stack of colorful, expensive envelopes and my mood starts to blacken. I loathe attending these parties and having to be fake with people. I don't even like attending my own company's holiday party. Most of these invitations come from the high rollers in the community and VIP clients. This pile is larger than previous years and there's no way I plan on attending most of them.

"I hate to remind you on how to do your job, but you need to go through these first and weed out the ones that aren't beneficial for us."

"Already did that, asshole," she grits out through clenched teeth, and I can tell she's one comment away from completely losing it on me.

"Why are there so many more this year?"

"More people decided that they want you to grace them with your heinous presence."

"I'm impressed that you're using big words this time when insulting me."

"Please have those piles ready for me in one hour," she demands before turning on her heel to leave and slamming my door shut after her.

I reluctantly start opening the invitations and begin the process of creating yes and no piles. After reading the third invitation, an idea springs to mind on how to get Ariana to go out with me. Most of these parties invite me and a guest to attend. Ari as my date gives us the opportunity to see each other outside of work and for her to start feeling more comfortable around me. *But how do I get her to agree to come with me?*

I need to present this to her as a business opportunity. I know money is tight for her and her family right now, so I could offer to pay her to be my date. Because the money would be going for her mother's medical bills, I don't feel like a complete douchebag for entertaining the offer. Ari refused to let me pay for a $5.00 cup of coffee, so I'm pretty confident that she's not interested in my money. I laugh out loud at the ridiculousness of this. Me, Warren Bentley, one of Chicago's most eligible bachelors, paying someone to attend some of the most elite holiday parties in the country. But if it gets her to say yes, then I would gladly pay any amount she demands.

Because Ari is priceless, and I refuse to take no for an answer.

I look at these invitations with a different mindset, searching for the ones that are the most fun and creative. Usually those are the parties I try to avoid at all costs, but Ari probably needs to have some fun in her life right now. I narrow my choices down to five parties that are all themed, one of them being a New Year's Eve masquerade ball. I make a list of specific wardrobe attire and presents I'll need ordered for these parties, and once satisfied, I grab the two piles and walk them over to Delilah's desk.

"Here are the ones I will attend and please RSVP for two people."

"Who is going with you?" She narrows her eyes at me, and I can just see her mentally going through a catalog of all my past conquests.

"I haven't decided yet," I lie, not ready to tell her about Ari. I'll wait to deal with the wrath of Delilah once Ari has confirmed she'll go with me. "Here's a list of presents and costumes I will need. Please email them to Ms. Leighton and let me know when she tells you they're ready so I can pick them up."

"The courier will grab them for you."

"No, I prefer to go to the store myself. I think it's high time I start visiting there more and making my presence known."

"I think that's unnecessary," she counters back, and I can tell she sees right through my bullshit. Delilah knows the store is low on my priority list of things at Bentley Corporation. It's why I pay our Chief Operation Office and Store Managers a lot of money to keep it running smoothly.

"I didn't ask for your opinion." I end the conversation with a nod and walk back to my office. I close the door behind me and sigh out in frustration. I hate being a dick to my sister, but sometimes she forgets who's in charge at work. I sit back down in my chair and swivel it around to look out my office window. While my view is mostly of a concrete jungle, I can see in the distance the roof of the store. My thoughts drift back to Ari, wondering if she's busy with a client right now or does she have the day off? Does she go to all of her mother's chemotherapy appointments? Does she have any food allergies? So many things to learn about her and I'm anxious to get started.

"I'm coming for you, Ari," I say out loud with a huge smile spread across my lips. The chase to win Ariana's heart won't be easy, but I never lose. She'll be mine even before she's ready to admit it.

Chapter Six

ARI

IT TOOK ME a couple of days to get everything off the list Delilah sent, but once all the presents were wrapped and his wardrobe was customized to his measurements, I was confident that Warren would be satisfied with my selections. I send Delilah an email about his items being ready for pick up and try to move on to focus on my upcoming appointment. I'm beyond excited to be working with stylist to the stars, Kellan Allen. Kellan is in town because one of his biggest clients, movie star Cal Harrington, lives here with his wife and children. Kellan needs a couple of dresses for Cal's wife to try on for a black-tie charity event they plan on attending.

"Are you nervous? Because I'm nervous for you!" Olivia dances into the office, trying to shake off her pent-up energy. "What if Cal Harrington comes with him? God, that man is so hot and that accent!" She picks up a sheet of paper and starts fanning herself. "He can read from the dictionary and I would probably come from the first word he pronounces."

I shake my head at her craziness. "You need to get laid just as badly as I do if that's all it takes. And no, I'm not nervous because for one thing, Cal Harrington is a human being just like you and I. Secondly, Kellan is picking up dresses for Cal Harrington's *wife*. So please keep all fantasies you have for him to yourself during Kellan's visit."

She sticks out her tongue at me and I laugh. "You're always so professional when we have VIP clients. Does anyone make you nervous?"

Warren does, but I refuse to tell her that. Olivia would have a field day if she knew what happened at the coffee shop and would tell everyone that we're probably going to get married. As much as I love her, she can be a little bit of a drama queen and loves to stir the gossip pot. She would question how I feel about him and quite frankly, I don't know what I feel. He makes my blood boil with frustration *and* desire.

"What's there to be nervous about? Again, they're human beings just like you and I."

"Except they have more money and can do more with it, which is not just like you and I." I chuckle at her accuracy and am about to agree when the notification alert from my emails draws my attention. I click open my inbox to see a response from Delilah.

"Oh shit," I say out loud, forgetting that Olivia is still in the office with me.

"What's wrong?"

"Mr. Bentley is coming to pick up his order, but I'll probably be in my meeting with Kellan. Can you handle this for me?"

"Of course I can. What time will he be arriving so I can make sure I freshen up to look my best self?" She wiggles her eyebrows up and down and I try to laugh, but on the inside, I feel sick to my stomach. Olivia is gorgeous with a charming personality and a vivacious figure. She's a magnet for men and I wouldn't be surprised if she peaks Warren's interest.

"He'll be here around 1:00 p.m."

"Okay, great. I wonder why he's coming here himself and not having us send his order by courier like we normally do?"

I was wondering the same thing, so I answer her with a shrug.

"Who knows, maybe he wants to check out how the store looks since we put up the holiday decorations." I write Delilah back with instructions for him to ask for Olivia instead of me, not giving her any details as to why. Five minutes goes by and the office phone rings.

"Why were you planning on avoiding me?" Warren questions through the phone, sending shivers up my spine at the sexy roughness of his voice. I want to hate the excitement that is bubbling inside of me, but I can't. I like that he's not happy about meeting with Olivia. Since Olivia is listening, I can't honestly answer his question, so I opt to add some extra dialogue to our conversation instead.

"Good morning, Mr. Bentley. I'm fine, thank you so much for asking. Yes, Olivia will have all your items available when you arrive. I apologize that I won't be able to see you myself. I'll be in a meeting with a scheduled client."

"Someone else is in the office with you, aren't they?" he asks in amusement.

"Yes, that's correct, sir." I respond, looking up to see Olivia watching me very closely.

"Good, because I have some serious questions to ask you, Ari, and I expect you to be one hundred percent honest with me. Do you understand?"

A pit forms in my stomach, not liking the mysterious tone in his voice or where this conversation might be heading. "Of course, Mr. Bentley."

"Excellent. Now, Ari, is it true you are attracted to me?"

What in the hell? "No, Mr. Bentley."

"I told you not to lie to me, Ariana. I saw the way you were staring at my lips as if you were a tiger ready to pounce on some red meat. So let me ask you again, are you attracted to me?"

Please God, kill me now. "Yes, Mr. Bentley," I whisper, looking up to see if Olivia heard me. Sure enough, her eyes are narrowed and to make things worse, she's getting up out of her chair and walking toward my desk. I turn down the volume on my phone to make sure she can't hear him through the receiver.

"Will you go out to dinner with me?" is his next question,

making my eyes bug out of my sockets.

Holy shit, Warren Bentley just asked me out. Me! Wait, why is he asking me out? Doesn't he realize we are polar opposites and that one tiny little detail that he's my boss?

"No, Mr. Bentley," I answer a little too firmly, causing Olivia to wave her arms around to get my attention.

"What's happening?" she whispers, and I place my finger over my mouth to shush her.

"I know you want to go out to dinner with me, Ariana, so therefore, you just lied to me again. Don't you realize there are consequences for your actions?"

I don't even want to know what he means by that. Okay, that's a lie. I *do* want to know what he means by that, because it's probably naughty. The *good* kind of naughty, but there is no way in hell I'm telling him. I'm probably just a new conquest for him, but *this* girl is not giving in. "Yes, Mr. Bentley."

"Every time you call me Mr. Bentley it brings up fantasies of the dirty things I want to do to you in one of the dressing rooms, so you might want to get used to calling me Warren."

I bite the inside of my cheek to prevent my mouth from dropping open. He's deliberately playing with me, knowing full well I can't call him Warren in front of a co-worker. I'm fuming on the inside...and incredibly turned-on. I will never look at dressing rooms the same now.

I can feel Olivia analyzing my red cheeks and I roll my eyes, pretending to be bored with the conversation. If Olivia sees any other kind of emotion from me, she'll know right away something's up. I clear my throat that suddenly became dry from thoughts of Warren doing wicked things to me in a dressing room. "Thank you, sir. Is there anything else I can help you with?" He laughs, causing me to clench my core at how yummy it sounds. This conversation needs to end before he says anything else that pushes my buttons, or makes me even more hot and bothered.

"What time will your appointment end?"

"It should take no more than an hour, sir."

"Tell Olivia she's no longer needed. I'll be there at two to see you. Oh, and Ari?"

"Yes, Mr. Bent—sir?" I correct, which only makes him chuckle.

Damn him and his sexy laugh that I want to hear again.

"Don't even think of coming up with some fake sickness that causes you to leave."

"Will do," I respond, my answer making him groan.

"I look forward to seeing you and that sassy mouth of yours, Ari." I don't even bother responding to that and hang up on him.

"What the hell was that all about?" Olivia demands, and I take in a deep breath, racking my brain to figure out what I'm going to tell her. There is no way in hell I can repeat *that* conversation to her.

"Oh, just Mr. Bentley being his usual douchie self. Thanks for being willing to meet with him for me, but he forgot some items on his list that he needs, so he's going to come in at two instead and we will finish up his order together." I can't even look at her when I'm lying because my poker face is lame and non-existent. I pretend to make up something to add to his list just in case she reads my handwriting.

"Oh boo, I was kind of hoping for some one-on-one time with the dashing Mr. Bentley," she says, and a mischievous idea comes to mind.

"Why don't you help me with him today?" I offer with a big smile, knowing full well Warren is going to be pissed at my antics.

"Are you sure?" She gives me a questionable look and I nod.

"Absolutely. He'll be so appreciative that we're both helping him out."

Olivia is beaming with excitement and I can't help but secretly be relieved to not be alone with him. There's something about Warren that puts me on edge. He's dangerously good-looking. Someone who's used to getting what he wants. I've seen his type before in law school and had no problems telling men like him to take a hike. But, for some reason, my brain refuses to tell him that, and I don't think it's because he's my boss. His apology to me the other day makes me wonder if there's another side to him. *Don't be fooled, Ari.* He probably sees me as another challenge.

I can't be distracted by foolish games and clearly, Warren Bentley is a huge distraction. My sole focus needs to be on my mother. If I'm being honest with myself, he's already become an interruption, and I'm afraid of the damage he might do if I let him weasel himself into my life.

My heart is already cracking from the idea that one day soon, my mother will no longer be with me. Getting involved with Warren Bentley would completely shatter it beyond repair.

Chapter Seven

WARREN

I MAKE SURE I arrive at the store at exactly two p.m. on the dot. I know there might be a chance that Ari is still with her client, but I didn't want to miss out on any time with her if she wasn't. I can only imagine the kind of excuses she would come up with to not see me if I happened to be late. Plus, I don't know if she has any more clients coming in for the day.

The store looks magnificent with the lavish holiday decorations that we put up every season, and I'm happy to see it is bustling with shoppers. I say hello to the workers who greet me as I walk by and take the escalators up to the second floor to the private offices of our personal shopping department. I'm pleasantly surprised to see Ari waiting for me in the small lobby. Unfortunately, she's not alone.

"Good afternoon, sir. I hope you've been having a great day so far." I notice her enthusiastic greeting and take note of the mischievous glint in her eye. She's up to something and I have no doubt it involves the woman standing next to her.

"My day just got better," I respond straight to Ari and openly admire her body, not caring whatsoever that the stranger is watching me closely. Ari looks very sophisticated today, wearing a black pant suit with black high heeled boots and gold jewelry. Her chestnut-colored hair is styled with half of it up and the rest falling in waves down her back. Her make-up is light but nevertheless accentuates her beauty.

She blushes at my blatant appreciation of her and clears her throat. "Mr. Bentley, have you met Olivia Hoover before? She's been in the personal shopping department for five years now. She will be assisting us today."

"Nice to meet you, Olivia." I nod my head at her, but turn my attention back to Ari. "I don't recall us needing assistance today." Ariana confirmed with Delilah that my order was ready, unless there was a miscommunication. For some reason, I highly doubt that and Ari is trying to avoid being alone with me.

"I figured Olivia can help us with ideas for the item you forgot."

"I didn't forget anything." I narrow my eyes at her and notice she shivers before looking away. I'm going to make this girl squirm in more ways than she has ever imagined.

"You didn't? I apologize, I must've misheard you. Olivia and I will be right back with your items then."

"Why don't I come with you and try some of the suits on to make sure they fit?" I smile wickedly as Ari's expression changes to one of a deer-in-the-headlights. *Two can play this game, little minx.* "Olivia, I actually do need to buy my sister a Christmas gift. I'm thinking she could really use a nice vacation. Maybe one of those fancy spas in Arizona or Palm Springs. Do you mind going to our travel concierge department and find out where they recommend?"

"Not a problem, sir."

"Excellent. Ari, show me to the dressing room," I tell her with a straight face, but I know she caught my wink. All color has drained from her face, and she's nervously wringing her hands while watching Olivia walk away from us.

"How about a tour of the office?" she suggests, and I chuckle at her efforts at stalling.

"Dressing room. Now, Ariana," I demand and she gulps before nodding her head. She turns around and I follow her down the hallway, my eyes glued to her sexy ass and the way her hips seductively sashay. She takes her keys out of her pocket as we approach dressing room four. I watch her hands shake as she attempts to fit her key in the lock. She inserts it after the third try, turns the lock and opens the door. She hits the light switch and walks briskly toward the back where the rack of clothes hang.

"Everything's here. What would you like to try on first?" Her back stiffens when she hears me lock the door. My footsteps are the only noise in the room. She turns just as I reach her and uses one of the suits as a shield between us. She presses it against my chest. "Why don't you try on your tux for the masquerade ball?"

Normally I would laugh at how adorable she's being, but I'm too turned on to think straight. The air is thick with our sexual tension and my eyes zone in on her parted lips. Her delicious scent of roses mixed with vanilla consume me and I know my control is about to snap. "I warned you about my thoughts on you and dressing rooms." I grab the suit by its hanger and hang it back on the rack to the left of her. I take that last final step, causing her breasts to come into contact with my chest.

She inhales a sharp breath and tries to step back, but she knocks into the clothes behind her. I've got her exactly where I want her and there's nowhere for her to run. "Olivia will be back momentarily," she whispers in warning. I hear the raspiness in her voice, see that her eyes are dilated, and I know she's just as turned on as I am.

"Then we better make the most of our time."

I don't give her a chance to respond and swoop in for a kiss. I start slow, gently touching my lips to hers. I go in for another and then another, each light peck becoming longer and longer. It's only after she opens her mouth to invite me in that I become more demanding. My tongue greedily accepts her warmth and I groan at how good she tastes, like apples and cinnamon. I knew she was going to taste sweet, but fuck if reality is far better than any fantasy I had. Her soft lips suck hungrily on mine as she nips them for more. My hands slide down her back and I cup her ass, bringing her against my hard-on. She grabs the lapels of my suit to hang on as her knees give out and I wrap one arm around her waist while my other hand grabs the clothing rack bar behind her to keep our balance. I start thrusting my tongue in and out of her mouth, imagining it was my dick inside of her. She snakes her arms up and around my neck, her hands crushing me to her. I groan as her pelvis starts rubbing against me. Her moans stroke the hardness of my cock, and I know if I let this continue, I won't be able to stop.

I will myself to slow down and break away from our kiss. Our heavy breathing fills the air and I swear it feels like it's a thousand degrees in here. "Fuck, I want you so badly, but if I didn't stop us then Olivia would see my hand deep inside your sweet, wet pussy, and then we'd really give her something to talk about." She hides her face in my chest and her groan makes me chuckle. I loosen my grip on her and let go of the bar. My hands immediately resume touching her, slowly stroking up and down her back. *Goddamn*, I love the way she immediately responded to me. Our chemistry is sizzling and my mind starts racing at how unbelievable sex is going to be with her. I know that won't be for a while and I'm willing to wait for however long that takes. My goal today was just to get her to agree to go out with me. I had no intentions of kissing her, but once we were alone together in this room and seeing how sexy she looked, I couldn't help myself. Now that I've had a taste of her, Ariana Leighton is off-limits to every other man for eternity.

I wait for her breathing to return to normal before breaking the ice again. "We have a lot to talk about. I will send my driver over at 5:00 p.m. to come get you and my order."

Her head snaps up, her cheeks flushed from desire. "We have nothing to talk about. This was a mistake."

I throw my head back and laugh. I let go of her and give her some space. "On the contrary, Ari. This was anything but a mistake. There will be much more where that came from." I turn around and walk to the door. I pull it open and look back at her. "Get used to this, Ariana, because this is only the beginning." I walk out of the dressing room without glancing back and head down the hallway to the lobby.

Olivia is coming off the escalator as I reach it. "Mr. Bentley, I have those suggestions for you."

"Just have Ari email them to me, please. Oh and Olivia, I left Ariana in a somewhat uncomfortable state back there. I know you're a good friend and will ask her what happened. I'm guessing she's going to lie to you out of embarrassment. The truth is that I kissed the shit out of her and hope to do it again soon." Her mouth drops open and she stares at me in shock. "I would appreciate your discretion and not spreading any gossip. I have a feeling once everyone finds out Ariana and I are going to be dating, they will give her a hard time. Your support and true friendship will be appreciated. Please keep me informed if anyone causes her trouble."

She blinks her eyes and slowly nods at me. "Su-sure."

"And any encouragement from you in my favor is also greatly appreciated." I give her a killer smile and wink, before taking off down the escalator.

Once Ari clears her mind, I know she'll arrive at my office with guns blazing and her iron clad wall up around her heart. She doesn't see herself the way I do. She thinks because we come from two separate worlds that we can't be together, but that's bullshit, and just an excuse to protect herself. I anticipate her refusing me again, so I need to come up with a fool-proof plan that she can't say no to.

Chapter Eight

ARI

I STEP OUT of the car and look up at the granite and marble building that houses Bentley Corporation with dread. I have no earthly idea what Warren thinks we need to talk about when I already said I will not go to dinner with him. My emotions since this afternoon's kiss have been like the needle of a seismograph that measures earthquakes, up, down and all over the damn place. His kisses lit my core on fire and if it wasn't for him stopping our kiss, I would've continued humping him like a dog in heat. Once reality seeped back into my brain cells, I was beyond embarrassed that what he told me he wanted to happen over the phone came true. I basically sucked the face off my too-hot-to-handle boss in one of *his* store dressing rooms. But then he left me confused when he said this is the beginning of us. There is no us, and there can't be. Here's a breakdown of why there can't be an us:

He's my boss. I'm his employee.

He's rich. I'm poor.

He's high society. I'm not even associated with any society.

He can have casual sex. I'm a clinger once anyone's penis is inside of me.

But the most important part of it all, his time is his to do with as he wishes, whereas I've committed mine to spending every free moment I can with my mother. I can't have a distraction like him take me away from her. Every day with her is so precious.

The last emotion he left me with was anger for telling Olivia what had happened between us. She grilled me like she was a prosecuting attorney and I was the prime suspect. When I told her every reason I had for not wanting to get involved with him, she looked at me as if I was crazy. "You know, for someone so intelligent, you're an idiot when it comes to men" I believe were her exact words.

Now here I stand a couple hours later, not wanting to go inside this building to see him. My lips still feel swollen from his kisses and my mind won't stop replaying what happened in the dressing room. I've never been kissed with such raw hunger before and it left me wanting more. I can't be thinking about things like his lips, or what sex would be like with him, or what he likes to do in his free time. I need to focus on my mom and this is exactly why I have my guard up. But every time my wall is in place, he tears it down with his wrecking ball. If he kisses me again, I know I'll agree to probably anything he asks of me.

"Mr. Bentley wants me to drive you home once you're done with your meeting, Miss Leighton." Sam, Warren's driver, says, interrupting my thoughts. "I'll be waiting for you right here whenever that time may be."

"That won't be necessary, Sam. I can take the train home."

"Mr. Bentley has insisted, ma'am."

"Of course he has," I mutter. I'll find another exit to sneak out of because there is no way in hell I want Warren to know where I live. I notice Sam walks back to the driver's side without unloading the items from the store. "Sam, can you help me carry Mr. Bentley's items up to his office?"

"There's no need to do that, Miss Leighton. I'll be taking them to his home later to drop-off."

"Oh, okay," I say in confusion. Of course Warren would

need his items at his house and not at the office. *What the hell am I even doing here?* I guess there's only one way to find out. Determined to get this over with, I head to the front entrance of the building and walk in.

"Can I help you?" asks the security guard at the desk. I've never been to the main Bentley Corporation offices before and the building decor is exactly what I pictured it to be, sleek, cold and modern.

"Yes, I'm here to see Warren Bentley." I give him my name before he calls Warren's office for confirmation. Once someone confirms my appointment, he hangs up, writes my name down and hands me a "visitor" tag with the date and time.

"Mr. Bentley's offices are located on the fifty-eighth floor. Take the escalator to your right up one floor to the elevators."

I thank him and follow his instructions. Once inside the elevator, I take a couple deep breaths and shake out the nervous energy from my hands.

Be strong, Ari. Do not fall into the Warren trance.

The elevator dings upon arrival and the doors open to reveal Delilah Bentley waiting for me.

"Good evening, Ariana." Her posture is stiff, and her smile does not reach her eyes. "I trust you're doing well."

"Hello, Ms. Bentley, I'm fine, thank you." I quickly scan my surroundings while greeting her. The office is surprisingly light and airy with gorgeous views of the city all around.

"Follow me and I will escort you to Mr. Bentley's office." Delilah turns on her heel and I'm left with no choice but to follow her through the maze of offices. Some heads lift up as we walk by, but for the most part, the ones who are working are concentrating on the task on hand.

The silence between Delilah and I as we walk only adds to my nervousness, so I decide to make small talk instead. "Have you had a good day today?"

She abruptly stops walking and turns to me. "Let's just cut through the bullshit. You shouldn't be here and I told my brother he needs to not entertain the idea of getting in your pants. Getting involved with you is a bad idea."

I'm momentarily taken aback by her bluntness.

"Why is that?" I ask, curious to hear her reasoning.

"You're an employee, Ariana! It's a human resources nightmare. If he does one thing wrong in your eyes, you can sue us."

Relief washes through me at knowing that's what she's concerned about and not because she thinks I'm some kind of gold-digger.

"I would never do that." I try to reassure her as we continue to walk.

"You say that now, but he hasn't done anything inappropriate for you to report him to HR."

So he hasn't told her about what happened today in the dressing room.

"Listen Delilah, I'm on the same page as you are. I know getting involved with Mr. Bentley is a terrible idea and I already turned down his dinner invitation."

She stops short again and looks at me in confusion. "You did? When?"

"Today when he was at the store."

This seems to confuse her even more. "Then why are you here?"

"Your guess is as good as mine. He asked that I deliver his items here, but then when we arrived, Sam informed me he was dropping them off at Mr. Bentley's house. I have no clue why I'm here."

She rolls her eyes and strides off, leaving me to walk briskly to catch up with her. "You're here because my brother doesn't take no for an answer when he wants something. And he certainly has his eyes set on you, Miss Leighton." She slows down as we get closer to a massive mahogany door. She stops in front of it and turns to me. "I like you Ari and as much as I love my brother, I don't want to see you get hurt. Be prepared that he will do whatever it takes to make you say yes. Good luck in there, you're going to need it." And with that, she knocks on the door and enters without waiting for his response.

"Ariana Leighton is here to see you, Warren. Friendly

reminder one last time that she's an employee and to *please* act professional." I awkwardly walk in and notice her giving him what must be her scary sister look before she turns to leave and shuts the door behind her.

I thrust my hands in my coat pocket, telling myself that they need to stay there throughout this whole meeting, because there is no touching *or* kissing allowed ever again.

I look around his office, needing a distraction. It's a huge office with a small conference table and chairs at one end, his desk in the middle and glass walls surrounding the entire office, showcasing the beautiful views of downtown Chicago.

"Hey you." He walks around his desk and comes toward me, his handsome smile devastating my heart to the point that I have to remind myself to breathe.

"Good evening, sir." I greet him professionally and keep my eyes focused on the view behind him, knowing that if I look him straight in his eyes, he'll ensnare me with his trance. This lasts for only for one second before he grabs my chin in between his fingers and forces me to look at him.

"Are you always this formal to men who've had their tongue down your throat?"

Gah, damn him and his sexy smirks!

I jerk my chin out of his reach and walk around him to his windows, needing to get as much space between us as possible. "What am I doing here, Warren?" I inquire while taking in the view of the city. It seems so calm and peaceful from here, a complete contrast to the turbulence that is going on inside me.

"You're here to drop off the items I ordered."

I turn around at his lie, placing my hands on my hips in anger. "Ha! You knew all along that wasn't the plan."

"Can you blame me for trying? I asked you out like a normal person would and you refused me."

"There's nothing normal about you, Warren."

"I'm taking that as a compliment."

"Of course you would," I mutter, sarcasm dripping from my tone. "I said no to dinner, Warren, and I mean it."

"But you don't really," he tells me with a shrug, making my

blood boil at how well he already knows me. "No one who kisses the way you kissed me means no."

"You. Kissed. Me." I point to him and then to me in exasperation.

He closes the distance between us in a few long strides, stopping only a couple of inches from me. "It doesn't matter who kissed who. What matters is how the chemistry between us is insatiable. Today was just a preview of what we're missing out on."

"Ah, I see. So you asked me out to dinner to try to be a gentlemen when all you want out of me is a quick fuck? How about you go fuck yourself instead," I say in anger and try to sidestep around him, but he grabs my bicep and pulls me back to where I was standing.

"I wouldn't fuck you quickly, Ariana. You're too special for that. I would slow fuck you with my tongue and then make passionate love to you with my dick. And not just once."

Desire slams into me and I clench my core tightly at how delicious his words sound. I can feel the anger rolling off him, but his eyes are heated with hunger. His gaze alternates between my eyes and my lips, making me wonder if he's going to kiss me again.

I want him to kiss me again, but I *need* him to stay away from me… and my heart.

"Why me?" I whisper in desperation, needing an answer. "We have nothing in common and come from complete opposite sides of the tracks. You can have any woman in the world. Why are you chasing me?"

"Why *not* you?" he questions back, his intense stare making me feel like he's searching for my soul. "Do you think it matters to me where you come from or how big your bank account is? You don't see your self-worth, do you, Ari? Well, let me tell you what I see."

Oh god, I don't want to hear any of this right now. I try to walk away from him, but he tightens his hold on me.

"I see a gorgeous woman who also happens to be intelligent, sassy, stubborn and witty. A woman who takes pride in everything she touches and has an impeccable work ethic. A person who cares about others, no matter what their social class is, and expects nothing in return." He grabs my chin again, forcing me to look at him. "I see a woman who gave up her dreams to take care of her dying mother."

I can't contain my gasp of surprise. *Olivia told him?* "How do you know about my mother?"

He moves his hand to cup my cheek. "It doesn't matter how I found out. What matters is that you need to start seeing how incredible you are."

"Anyone would've done what I did."

"No, they wouldn't have. Trust me, I know."

I shake my head against his palm. "You don't know anything."

"My mother died when I was sixteen of the exact same cancer your mother is battling."

I inhale sharply, not expecting that. I had heard his mother passed away when he was young, but no one mentioned how. Tears spring to my eyes and before I can blink them away, one slips out, and Warren swipes the pad of his thumb over my cheek to dry it away. I'm having a hard time dealing with this at twenty-seven; I can't even imagine how much harder it would've been at sixteen. My heart hurts for Warren and his sister.

"You don't have to go through this alone, Ari."

His words are sweet, and normally, I would be ecstatic that this is happening to me, but there is nothing normal about this situation. I smile sadly at him and shake my head. "I can't have any distractions in my life right now, Warren. Work and my mother need my full attention."

"What if you didn't need to work so much right now? What if I helped cover her medical expenses and you take time off?"

"What?" I shrink away from him, surprised by his suggestion. "Why? Why would you do that? We barely know each other." Then it dawns on me what he's really suggesting. "I understand now. I understand all this now. You want to pay her medical bills so I can *owe* you something. Something like sex, maybe? Or maybe you need something in your privileged life that will make you feel better about yourself?" He starts to shake his head no, but I don't let him get a word in. "Find someone else to be that for you, Warren. I'm *not* your charity case."

"Damnit, Ariana, that's not what I meant," he growls out in irritation. He drops his hands from me and rakes one of them through his hair in frustration. That's when I take my chance to leave and head straight for the door.

"Just leave me alone, Warren," I plead over my shoulder at him.

"I can get her into Blackburn."

His words halt me in my tracks and steal my breath away. I whip around to stare at him, needing to see with my own eyes if he's being serious. The Blackburn Institute is a private clinic that combines holistic and modern medicine to treat patients who are in stages three and four of various cancers. You apply to get in and if accepted, stay for a minimum two weeks. The cost is exuberant and something my family could never afford.

I narrow my eyes, searching his face for any signs that this might be some twisted, cruel joke, but all I see is sadness as he comes closer. "My mother went there twice. Each time for a three week stay. I believe they prolonged her life by a couple of years."

That is what every review I read said about the Blackburn Institute. That whatever they do there seems to help slow the spread of the cancer. Getting her in would be a dream come true. One that I would even sell my soul for.

Warren reads my emotions, sees the questions in my eyes. "I will make the call tomorrow. All you have to do in return is agree to be my date to no more than five holiday parties I have to attend. I'll provide your wardrobe," he states quickly when he sees me about to interrupt. "No strings attached. No sex. Not even kissing. If you want either one, then you will be the initiator."

"What's in this for you?" I question, still not understanding why he would do this for me when we're practically strangers.

"I get to spend time with you, and you get to see the real me. Not the Warren Bentley you read about in the gossip columns."

"And what if after these parties, I don't want to see you

anymore?"

"I highly doubt that will be the outcome, but if some alien snatches your soul from your body in the middle of the night and you still decide you don't want to ever see me again, I will honor your request and leave you alone."

He's trying to lighten the mood with a joke, but this is no laughing matter to me. Spending alone time with Warren is just going to make me fall for him and it will tear my heart when I have to tell him goodbye. *If* I agree to this insane idea of his. *Who am I kidding?* I would be a fool not to accept his offer. I would take the broken heart if it gave me more time with my mother.

"I want this all in writing. I will think about this while your lawyer drafts up a contract."

My heart skips a beat as he gives me one of his panty-melting smiles and nods his approval. "You'll have it in your email within three days."

I nod curtly at him before spinning around to leave. I need to get the hell out of here before I give Warren Bentley any other part of me.

DELILAH BENTLEY

THE DOOR TO Warren's office jolts open, and Ariana comes out of there like a tornado. I jump up from my seat when I notice she's on the verge of tears.

"Ariana, are you okay?" I make my way around my desk but she holds up her hand to stop me from coming near her. She nods her head and practically runs down the corridor. I don't bother to call after her as it's clear she wants to be alone. Anger at my brother starts to rise from the pit of my stomach. I march straight into his office and slam his door behind me.

"What the hell did you do to her, Warren? She just ran out of here looking miserable." His back was to me when I walked in and when he slowly turned around, I gasped in surprise at the sadness on his face.

"Sit down, Delilah, so I can tell you the whole story and maybe, just maybe, you'll stop making assumptions of your little brother."

I watch him pull out his desk chair, sit down and rub his eyes with the palm of his hands. He looks worn out and I start to worry. I gulp down my questions and sit in the chair across from him, ready to listen and put my judgement aside.

For the next hour, Warren tells me everything about Ariana Leighton. How they met, how he felt when he met her, what our grandmother told him, the day at the coffee shop and finally today. I stare at him in awe as he finishes, seeing my brother in a totally new light.

"I feel and sound like a lunatic, but Delilah, I can't stop thinking about her. Obviously, I'm physically attracted to her, but it's her heart that I want." He shakes his head and chuckles. "I don't know. I just feel like she's it for me. It's the oddest fucking feeling in the world, but one I've never been so sure of."

I've never seen or heard my brother act like this and I internally get emotional over it, because I know our mother would be so proud of him. She loved us fiercely and she was always worried that Warren would turn out to be cold like our father. He seems to have proven us both wrong.

"I will do everything in my power to help you win her heart," I tell him, my tone sincere, letting all my previous objections go to the wayside. My brother's happiness is my number one priority, and I'll do whatever it takes to make sure that happens.

"That's my girl," he says with a slow smile that lights up his entire face. He fills me in on what's going to happen next and we start planning together.

Chapter Nine

ARI

I AVOID WORK and Warren for the next thirty-six hours. Conveniently, it was my day off the following day after meeting with him and I was so relieved it worked out that way. I was physically and emotionally drained and all I did was lay on the couch and watch movies with my mother. She knew something was wrong with me as soon as I came home the night before and went straight to bed without eating dinner. I didn't come out of my room until the following morning. She tried to get me to talk to her, but I wasn't ready. I didn't want to think about Warren's or my mother having cancer. All I wanted to do was get lost in some fictional world. When she stopped her badgering and agreed to watch movies with me, I demanded no romantic comedies or dramas that contained death. That little hint was all my mother needed to not ask any more questions.

"Are you sure it's okay for you to leave work early to take me to chemo?" my mother asks the next morning over breakfast. I'm once again running late for work, since I forgot to set my alarm due to falling asleep earlier than is normal for me.

"You're my mother, of course it's going to be okay. And if it's not, they can go fuck off."

"Language, Ariana," she warns in her stern, motherly voice.

I shake my head and smile, giving my mom an exaggerated eye roll. Only she would chastise me at twenty-seven about cursing. "Sorry... but not really because I have no problems telling them that if they do."

"Ariana, you need to be grateful to have a job."

"I *am* grateful. I never said I wasn't."

"Good, so please don't tell your boss to fuck off then."

Little too late for that. "Language, Mother," I warn right back, giving her a dose of her own medicine. She laughs and the sound is music to my soul. I need to record her laughing so I never forget how wonderful it sounds. The idea of never hearing it again turns my mood to sadness and my thoughts turn back to Warren's offer. I can't really accept it without talking to her first. I pull out my phone and text Olivia to let her know that I'll be late.

"Mom, I need to talk to you about something that's been going on," I start, once I see Olivia's texts with a thumbs up.

"About damn time. Dealing with your grumpy butt last night was almost as bad as chemo," she jokes, but it's hard for me to smile at her since I don't find that funny.

"Sorry about that. I've just had a lot on my mind and wanted a night not to think about anything."

"What's going on, honey?" She places her hand over mine and squeezes, her eyes filled with worry as she gazes at me.

"Well, I've met someone and he has completely overwhelmed me. Any rational thoughts I used to have are completely gone because of him." Tears of happiness spring to her eyes as she laughs. She covers her mouth with her hands and looks at me as if I just told her I won the lottery. "Don't get too excited, Mom. There's a lot of obstacles that stand in our way and I honestly don't think it would be a good idea to be with him."

"What kind of obstacles?" she asks, her brow furrowed in confusion.

"For one, he's a notorious playboy."

"Ooh," she says slowly, her smile fading like I knew it would. No mama wants their baby dating a manwhore. "Well, maybe being with you will change his ways."

I give her a doubtful look. "Another factor is he's filthy rich and runs in high society circles."

"And that makes you uncomfortable because we aren't?" she questions, and I slowly nod at her. "So you're discriminating against him because he has money?"

"Well, no. I just don't want people to think we're only together because I'm after his money."

"Since when do you care what other people think?"

"I usually don't, but for some reason with him, I care."

"But that's not very fair to him. Have you gone out with him yet?"

I give her a sheepish look and grimace. "No."

"Has he asked you out?"

"Yes."

"What excuse did you give him for turning him down?"

"That dating my boss would be a very bad idea."

Her eyes widen and her mouth drops in surprise. "Warren Bentley asked you out?"

"Shocking, right?"

"Not in the way you're thinking, Ariana. You're a beautiful, intelligent woman. Any man, including Warren, would be lucky to have you."

"You're supposed to say that, you're my mom." I roll my eyes at her and am rewarded with her smacking me on the head.

"So then what happened?"

"He's now blackmailing me into going out with him."

"Blackmail? How?"

"Well, he first offered to pay all of your medical bills if I attend five holiday parties with him, including buying my wardrobe." Her mouth falls open in shock but doesn't last long before a big, wide smile spreads across her face.

"Oh my gosh, that's so romantic. It's like you're Julia Roberts in *Pretty Woman*."

"Yeah… except last time I checked I *wasn't* a prostitute!"

She groans out her frustration at me while I glare at her. "Mom, I can't believe you would be okay with me repaying him back with sex."

"First off, I never said anything about sex. Secondly, he's an extremely attractive man, so I would hope you would want to have sex with him. I mean, if I was your age and single, I would've gone out with him already and gave it up probably on the first date with the way that man looks."

"La, la, la, la! I don't want the mental image of you and him in my brain." I yell out with my index finger in my ears, acting like a complete two-year-old because it's making her laugh. I shiver, grossed out while thinking of my mom and dad having sex. Yes, obviously I'm alive so I know she's had it with him, but still... gross.

"You're so ridiculous." She sighs. "Anyway, I'm blown away by the generosity of his offer. You turned him down, right?"

"Of course I did." I got my pride from her, so I knew she wouldn't want me to accept his donation. "But he came back with an even better offer if I go out with him."

"What could be a better offer than that?"

"Getting you an all-expenses paid trip to the Blackburn Institute."

She gasps and places her hand over her heart. "Oh my god."

I smile sadly at her and grip her free hand. "I'm going to accept that offer."

Tears fill her eyes and slowly start to slip down her cheeks, causing my own eyes to water up. "Ari, no," she whispers, shaking her head. "You don't need to accept any offer from him. If you like him, then you should go out with him, no strings attached."

"I do like him, but he's going to completely break my heart."

"You don't know that. If anything, you might break his heart if you push him away."

"Mom, he can have any woman in the world. I'm a nobody! Clearly he just wants sex."

"Don't you *ever* call yourself a nobody, Ariana Rose Leighton, and you don't know that. Why wouldn't he want you for *you*?"

"I'm going to accept his offer," I repeat as I start to cry, not wanting to believe that she might be right.

"Ari, baby." We both stand up and she pulls me in a tight embrace. "Sweetie, I'm dying no matter what. Your decision to go out with him shouldn't be based on me, but on how you feel for him. Don't let his money or him being your boss stop you from missing out on what could be the love of your life." She pulls back and cups my face while wiping away my tears with her thumb. "Don't miss out on life because of me. Don't you understand that your happiness is what matters to me the most?"

I nod and smile through my tears at her. "I know, Mom. But if they can help keep you with me for just a little bit longer, then I'm accepting his offer. I'll even take after you and have sex with him after the first date as a thank you."

That breaks the mood and we both start to laugh. She grabs a napkin off the table and starts dabbing my cheeks to wipe up the mascara that has run down my face.

"You're going to need to reapply your make-up before you leave." She kisses my forehead and rests her own against mine. "Promise me, Ari, that you will think about what I said."

"I promise. I love you, Mom."

"I love you more." I smile at her usual response and pull away from her arms to get ready for work.

CHRISTINE BENTLEY

THE RINGING OF my cell phone jolts me out of my sleep. I reach over to grab it and concern fills me when I see Angela Leighton's name flashing on the screen.

"Angie, are you okay?" I answer, praying that she's not calling me from the hospital.

"Did I wake you? Oh I'm so sorry, I don't know what time it is there."

"No, it's all right," I reassure her, needing to know if she's ok. "Tell me what's happening?"

"Oh, I'm fine, but I had to call you because I just talked with Ariana. You're right, *it's happening!*"

The excitement in her voice makes me smile and I sit up in anticipation. "Tell me what she said."

For the next thirty minutes, Angie tells me her whole conversation and what has been transpiring between Warren and Ariana since I've been gone. My heart bursts with pride when she tells me Warren is going to get Angie into the Blackburn Institute.

"Christine, I need you to talk to him. His offer is too much and makes me feel uncomfortable."

I have zero plans on talking my grandson out of his offer. "Angie, what's the point in having all this money if we can't do good things with it? I'm not talking to Warren and that's final."

"But—"

"End of discussion, Angie. Do this for your daughter... and for me." The line goes quiet and I at first think she has hung up on me, but then I hear a sniffle and know that she's still there.

"Thank you, Christine. For being my friend and for wanting what's best for my family."

"I'm so grateful for our friendship, Angie. You helped me during one of my darkest periods and I'm here to do the same for you."

I fill her in on my vacation so far and we end the conversation with her promising me an update next week on Ari and Warren. I place my cell phone back on my nightstand and settle into my covers again.

"Well done, my boy," I say out loud with love, so proud of Warren and the man that he's become. I just hope Ariana gives him a fair chance.

Chapter Ten

ARI

SINCE I WAS already going to be late for work, Olivia asked me to grab us both coffees on the way in. Because it's a chemotherapy day for my mom and I'm taking her instead of my dad, he left us his car so she doesn't have to be exposed to germs on public transportation. I love when I get to drive to work instead of taking the train. I feel like I have my freedom back when I drive, and some days, I just want to get on the highway and keep driving. I hate that I don't have my own car anymore, but I needed to sell it in order to help out with the medical bills. One day I will get another car, but for now, we need to stay a one car family. His car is paid off and he takes great care of it to make sure we can get a couple more good years out of it.

Fortunately, I'm only running late to work by ten minutes because I don't have to take the train, so I oblige Olivia and stop at the coffee shop. Since morning rush hour is over, the shop is pretty much empty, with the employees cleaning up and getting ready for the lunch crowd.

"There she is! Where have ya been, Miss Ari?" Mrs. Johnston

asks when I approach the counter. I haven't been in since that day with Warren, not because I was scared that he would show up again, but I've been trying to spend less money here and save it for some last-minute Christmas gifts for my parents.

"Sorry, Mrs. Johnston, been busy."

"I hope you've been busy with that hunk of a man who was with you last time." She shouts out my usual order and pushes some buttons on her register.

I don't respond to her and instead smile while handing over my credit card. She doesn't take it and looks at me in confusion. "Why are you trying to give that to me?"

Oh no, is Mrs. Johnston ill? "To pay for my order," I remind her slowly, my eyes searching hers in concern. Her eyes look clear and present, not like she's in a far away mental land.

She stares at me for a second longer before a knowing smile spreads across her face. "You don't know, do you?"

"Know what?" Now I'm really getting nervous that she's going to deliver bad news. I can't bear anymore sadness.

"Hottie in the suit set up a house account for you. Said he wanted you to think of him every time you drank your coffee and ate your scone. He also bought a $1000 gift card for Dale and told me to replenish it when it gets to zero on him." She points over my shoulder and I turn to see Dale, my homeless man, sitting in the corner drinking a large cup of coffee with two of his friends who also look homeless. My eyes widen from the shock as I take in his brand-new coat. It was one of the ones I picked out for Warren per his list. Dale sees us looking at him and he lifts up his coffee cup.

"Hey crazy lady! Happy holidays to you and your boyfriend! Thanks for helping us keep warm." The other two men turn around, raise their cups and shout out their thanks.

I smile and wave at them, but can barely see through the tears that have filled my eyes. I turn back to Mrs. Johnston in shock since I had no idea Warren had done this. "Wow," I whisper in awe of his generosity. "When did this happen?"

"He came in over the weekend to set up your account and buy the gift card. Dale told me about his new coat yesterday. Can I ask you a question, sweetheart?"

"Sure," I answer, still in disbelief over what I just learned.

"Why are you not with loverboy? Is he a bad guy or something?"

"No, he's not," I tell her with a shake of my head. "It's just complicated, Mrs. Johnston."

My order is placed next to her and she hands my coffee and scone to me. "Honey, it's only as complicated as you make it."

I give her a half smile in acknowledgment. "Thank you, Mrs. Johnson." Not wanting to stick around and have her psychoanalyze my reasoning for not dating Warren, I say goodbye to her and Dale before leaving.

Mrs. Johnston's words stay with me until I get to my office. I park the car in the employee lot behind the building and make my way in. Olivia is on the phone when I arrive and I'm grateful she's distracted. I put my belongings away and try to focus on work. I have a lot to do today before taking my mother to her appointment, and I want to accomplish everything on my to-do list.

I log into my email and start responding to the first one when my desk phone rings. I see it is Delilah Bentley calling and I inwardly groan, hoping this is a work-related call and has nothing to do with Warren.

"Good Morning, Ari," she says after I answer. "I wanted to get your personal email from you so I can send over the contract you requested from Warren."

"Oh, sure," I respond hesitantly, trying to disguise my surprise at her knowing about the contract. I give her my email and remain silent, waiting for her to end the call.

"I hope you don't mind, but Warren confided in me about everything and well, I just want to say—" She hesitates, and her gulp is audible. "—that if you ever need someone to talk to who understands what you're going through, please don't hesitate to reach out to me."

"Thank you, Ms. Bentley," I answer softly in appreciation.

"Oh, please call me Delilah. I'm really hoping you and I become good friends since we'll be seeing more of each other."

"Will we?" I question innocently, even though I know *exactly* what she's implying.

"You know we will, Ari." She laughs and I can't help but smile at the sound. I've enjoyed working with Delilah and a part of me wants her friendship. "I will also include Warren's cell phone number in the email. He asked me to tell you that he looks forward to hearing from you once you've read over the terms of the contract."

I bet he does. "I will look it over when I can, and get back to him," I tell her. We exchange a couple more pleasantries and end the call.

My fingers itch to open my personal email now, but I don't want to do that on a work computer. Besides, it would be good to make Warren wait a little. He knows he has me exactly where he wants me and I can only imagine the satisfaction he will feel when he sees my signature on this contract.

I pick up my coffee cup and smile before taking a sip. It was incredibly sweet of him to not only set up an account for me at the coffee shop, but to take care of Dale and provide him with a new coat. That unsuspected act of kindness warms my heart and I sigh deeply. He knows how to put me in a Warren trance even when he's not around.

You've got it bad, Ari.

Yeah, I do.

Sighing again, I shake my head to clear my thoughts. It's time to focus on work since my hours are limited. I'll deal with my feelings for Warren Bentley later.

As soon as we get back from my mother's chemotherapy appointment, I hole myself up in my room, turn on my laptop and read the contract. It's a pretty standard contract and the terms are exactly as we discussed in his office, including the part of no sexual activity unless initiated by me. I'm not really surprised to see it there, but nevertheless, it still made me laugh and a blush stings my cheeks when I remember our kiss.

I yearn for more of those kisses.

Will I really be able to abstain from kissing him once we start spending time together?

Looks like you're going to find out, Ari.

I insert my electronic signature into the contract, save a copy for my records and email it back to Delilah to give to Warren. Before I close my email, I program his number into my cell phone and turn off my computer.

I check in on my mom and heat up leftover spaghetti for dinner. After dinner is eaten and the dishes are done, Mom gets ready for bed while Dad sits in his recliner and watches the news. I try to concentrate on the book I'm reading, but my mind keeps going back to Warren. I check my email on my phone, waiting to see if I hear back from him or Delilah, but so far, no response. I wonder if I should text him letting him know I sent it back.

Maybe you just want an excuse to talk to him.

No, I'm just being courteous and respectful.

My internal debate lasts for a couple minutes longer before I finally get up the courage to text him. I say goodnight to my parents and head upstairs to my bedroom for some privacy.

Me: Are you available to talk?

I realized I forgot to identify myself when I sent the text. I'm about to say it's me when he responds first.

Warren: I'm always available for you, Ariana.

Me: How did you know it was me?

Warren: Inserts Side Eye Emoji

I roll my eyes and shake my head because I can just envision that wicked smirk of his.

Me: I really should report you to Human Resources.

Warren: You would never and in my defense, Delilah had it. You gave it to her when you first became our shopper.

Shit, he's right. I did give it to her all those years ago. I don't even think she's ever used it. I decide not to acknowledge he's right by getting to the point of why I am texting him.

Me: I emailed back the signed contract. Please let me know the schedule and times of the parties so I can make sure they are on my calendar and that I get off of work at an

appropriate hour in order to get ready.

Warren: I will send you a detailed schedule tomorrow, along with the dress code for each party.

Ugh, I forgot about the wardrobe part.

Me: I really don't feel comfortable with you buying my wardrobe for these functions. I'm sure I have appropriate attire in my closet.

I know for a fact that I *don't* have anything appropriate, especially for the black-tie events, but maybe I can borrow something from Olivia, who I'm sure does.

Warren: It was stated in the contract that you just signed. Didn't peg you for one to breach contracts so quickly.

I narrow my eyes at this, knowing full well he's trying to rile me up.

Me: Watch it, or I'll embarrass you by picking out dresses that leave little to the imagination.

Warren: You do that and I will be the one breaching the contract by initiating sexual activity.

I shiver in delight when memories of feeling Warren's hard-on in the dressing room spring to mind. Even through our clothes, I could tell he was big and the friction of rubbing up against him makes my core clench in need. I have to change the subject and keep it PG rated.

Me: I stopped by the coffee shop today. You really didn't need to set up an account on my behalf. I can pay for my own breakfast.

Warren: I have no doubt you can, but I like doing nice things for others. Don't you?

God, he's good. The man can infuriate and charm you all in the same breath. He should've been a lawyer.

Me: What you did for Dale was beyond generous. He was smiling and seemed elated today. Thank you for making him happy.

Warren: I want to make you happy if you let me.

I hold my breath at his words, not knowing how to respond.

Is this really happening? I want this to be real, but I'm so scared.

Warren: I didn't mean to make you uncomfortable or push you. Just being honest and real with you. I'm happy you reached out to me tonight.

Me: Thank you for being honest. I hope you always will be with me. Thank you again and I'll make sure I'm ready for the first party on Friday. Goodnight, Warren.

Warren: Sweet dreams, Ariana. I hope you dream of me like I know I'll be of you.

I close my eyes and take a deep breath, praying that I did the right thing by signing that contract. I get ready for bed and drift off to the images of my blue-eyed devil who most certainly does delicious things to me in my dreams.

Chapter Eleven

WARREN

I TAP MY fingers against my bouncing knee, watching the outside world speed by as Sam drives us to Ari's house. The pent-up nervous energy coursing through me at seeing her again confirms to me that this is not just lust I'm feeling. I've *never* been nervous at seeing a woman before and I've been with my fair share of them. If anything, they're always the ones nervous around me. If Ariana is nervous to see me, she won't dare show it. The little minx will probably turn up her adorable little nose and try to ignore me.

I still can't believe I had to blackmail a woman into going out with me. I chuckle at the irony. Women throw themselves at me and the one woman I want more than anyone else could walk away with my heart in her back pocket and she doesn't even realize it. I have to make the most of these next two weeks with her. Going to a holiday party together is not my idea of a great first date, but she left me with no choice. I smile at the images of her playing on repeat in my mind. I'm excited to see her and to prove to her how right we are together.

"We're almost there, sir," Sam informs me, and I'm relieved to see she only lives fifteen minutes away from the store, making her commute to work bearable. It's been a couple of days since I'd seen her, but I've made sure to text her every day, asking how she was and just trying to get her used to hearing from me. I was delighted to see her initiate our text conversation last night when she sent me a message first to say good night. I was still at the office working, but managed to keep our conversation going for another thirty minutes. After tonight, we're moving forward with phone calls instead of this texting bullshit.

Five minutes later, we turn off the main road and onto a residential street. We pull up to the curb and stop in front of an older, modest, two-story, light brick house with a huge bay window on the main floor. I shake my head at Ariana's earlier nonsense about her not wanting me to see her house. This is a beautiful, well-kept neighborhood that she has nothing to be ashamed about. Living in a shack couldn't make me want her any less.

I instruct Sam to keep the car running, grab the flowers I brought, and get out to retrieve Ari. I'm halfway up the walkway when her door opens, and she steps outside. I can't tell what she's wearing yet due to her winter coat covering her up, but her hair and make-up look flawless. She looks gorgeous and it's going to be hard to keep my hands to myself. I'm also going to have to keep my temper in check tonight because I know the men at the party will be eyeing her.

Her eyes widen at the bouquet of flowers I'm holding, a surprised smile touching her lips. "You didn't have to bring me flowers," she says as I get closer to her.

"I didn't. These are for your mother." I pull the other bouquet of flowers I was holding out from behind my back. "This one is for you."

Her mouth drops open, and it takes all my will power not to grab her and kiss it closed. "You brought my mother flowers?"

I shrug in response, not seeing what the big deal is. "Of course. Don't you think they'll make her happy?"

She stares at me a little longer before clearing her throat

and shifting her gaze back to the flowers. "That's really nice of you, thank you. Let me go bring these inside real quick." She turns halfway around before stopping and looking at me with narrowed eyes. "You stay here."

"That's really rude of you to leave me out here freezing in the cold. I'm sure your mother wouldn't approve," I tease, knowing full well that Ari has no intentions of inviting me inside. A movement in the window catches my eye and I see Mrs. Leighton trying to hide behind the curtain. I walk toward the window and decide to have a little fun with her as well.

"Hello, Mrs. Leighton," I greet in a loud voice, hoping she can hear me through the glass. I can tell she's giggling as she waves hello. "I look forward to the day your daughter invites me inside to introduce myself properly to you." I smile as she covers her mouth in laughter. She turns around at something Ari says, and I watch her place a hand over her heart. She turns back to me and mouths, "Thank you, they're beautiful" regarding the flowers. I bow in acknowledgement and yell, "You're welcome. I'll have Ari back before midnight." I wave goodbye to her as I turn to wait for Ariana to come back out.

"I'm not twelve you know, you don't have to tell my mother when you're bringing me back," she grumbles after slamming her front door.

"Better to tell her I'm bringing you back then not at all, unless you're going to approve of a sleepover?" I wiggle my eyebrows at her before grabbing her hand and winding my fingers through hers. I grip her tightly so she doesn't try to pull away. She rolls her eyes at me while I lead us to the car.

"You're incorrigible," she mutters as I open the door for her to get in.

"Ah, but you didn't say no."

She gets in the car and reaches for the door handle. "No!" she says firmly and shuts the door in my face. I laugh while walking around the back of the car and get inside.

"All set to go, Sam," I tell him, and he nods. He drives the car away from her house and we're off to our first party.

"So, give me the scoop on tonight and where we're going,

please." I grin at how uncomfortable she looks sitting plastered against the doorframe, making sure she's as far away from me as possible.

"We're going to Bert Griffith's holiday party at his house."

"Who's that?"

"Just the owner of one of the largest investment groups in Chicago."

"Oh, so no big deal whatsoever," she says, her voice dripping with sarcasm, making me chuckle.

"Right. It'll be stuffy, pretentious, and downright boring. His house is magnificent though. I thought you might enjoy it and see how suburbia life is."

She looks at me oddly before responding. "Why do you go if you think the parties are boring?"

"We are in business together. It's out of courtesy. I bring him this very expensive bottle of whiskey as a present, I say hello to his guests, and then I leave."

"So we'll be back home pretty early then?" Is that faint disappointment I hear in her voice? I hope so.

"Not really. It takes over an hour to get there."

"What?" She looks out the window to try to assess our surroundings. "Where does he live?"

"Winnetka and we're in rush hour traffic." She groans and throws her head against her headrest. "I can think of plenty of things to pass our time, but all of them would breach our contract, so instead, let's play the question game."

She gives me a skeptical look before sighing out loud. "Fine, but let's not make every question a sexual one, okay?"

"Why does everything have to go back to sex with you?" I jest, causing her to throw the gloves she recently took off at me. "Thanks for the souvenir," I laugh and put her gloves in my pocket. "All right, let's begin. Ladies first."

"I can ask any question I want?"

"Yes, provided it isn't sexual per your rules."

"Have you ever had a serious girlfriend before?"

I laugh at her getting straight to the point and not holding anything back. "I had a fiancée once, does that count?" I joke, then grin at her shocked expression.

"Really? When did you guys break up?"

"About five years ago. She was only with me for my name and money."

"I'm sorry," she whispers, and genuinely looks it.

"Don't be, because if it worked out, we wouldn't be in this car together right now."

"I would hope not."

"Ok, my turn." I pretend to think of a question, but I've already had one on my mind. "If money wasn't an object, what would you be doing with your life?"

"Finding a cure for cancer," she says with no hesitation and a sad smile. I completely believe she would too. I want to reach out and hug her so badly. This being a gentleman and shit is annoying when all I want to do is ravish her and throw out her stupid rules.

"Is Delilah your only sibling?"

"Yes, and she's enough."

I love the sound of her laughter, and I'm determined I'll do anything, including walking in a dress down Michigan Avenue, to hear her do that again.

We continue asking each other questions and before long, we arrive at the Griffith estate. Sam drops us off at the gate and I gently place my hand at the small of Ari's back to lead her to the front entrance. We follow some other guests inside the house where we're greeted by a butler, who takes our coats for us once we've removed them. My dick hardens at the sight of how hot Ari looks in her dress. It's a stylish cocktail dress with nothing revealing about it, but the maroon velvet dress clings perfectly to her curves. The sleeves have a stylish slit up to her elbows, revealing gold bracelets on her delicate wrists.

"You look beautiful," I whisper in her ear, thoroughly enjoying the blush that taints her cheeks.

"Warren!" Bert Griffith says in a boisterous voice. "So glad you made it." His eyes immediately zoom in on Ari with interest. "And whom might this lovely creature be?"

Creature... as if she's something other than human? Why do people say such stupid shit?

I notice Ari's tight smile and I wonder if she's thinking the exact same thing. I wrap my arm around her waist and bring her against my side.

"This is my girlfriend, Ariana. Ari, this is Bert Griffith." I bite the inside of my cheek to keep from laughing out loud at the look she shoots me for calling her my girlfriend. I know she wants to refute that title, but instead, she locks her jaw and keeps her fake smile plastered on her face.

"Nice to meet you, Mr. Griffith," she says while shaking his hand.

"Likewise and please call me, Bert." He turns his attention back to me and gives my arm a light punch. "You little devil, I didn't realize you were seeing someone serious."

I hand him his gift and slap his arm lightly back. "That's right, call the press. Warren Bentley is off the market." Bert and I laugh at my joke, but I don't think Ariana finds it quite funny. She smiles politely at us with one of those *What in the hell am I doing here* expressions.

"Well, please, come in and enjoy yourselves. Buffet is in the main dining room but please feel free to roam the house. All we ask is that you please don't christen our guest rooms." He nudges my side with a wink and leaves us to greet his other guests.

"I can't believe he just said that," Ari mutters while keeping her smile in place.

"See why we won't be staying long?" I nod to an acquaintance and lean down to Ari's ear. "Let's go get a drink. There's a couple of people I have to say hello to. We'll mingle, grab a bite, take a tour of the house and then leave. Sound good?"

"Lead the way."

We make our way to the bar and I learn that Ari is not a wine girl, but prefers vodka soda with lime. She barely eats any of the food at the buffet and is able to keep up constant chatter with anyone who talks to her. I observed that she has this magnificent ability to get people to deflect from asking her questions and instead, focuses on them, asking intelligent questions that require lengthy responses.

She really would make a brilliant lawyer.

We take a tour of the house and I can tell she's impressed with it, but gives no indication if this is the kind of house she dreams of living in. "So, what do you think?" I ask her when we're outside on the heated patio.

"About what?"

"The house?"

"The view is incredible."

"Yes, but could you imagine yourself living in a house like this?"

She's thoughtful for a moment before answering. "It's a gorgeous house, but entirely too big. Why do two people need a nine-bedroom house?"

"My thoughts exactly." Her answer doesn't surprise me. Ari is a no-frills kind of girl. She's still sophisticated, but in her own way. Materialistic items don't impress her, but she doesn't judge anyone who does like them. It so fucking refreshing and turns me on even more. I don't have to impress her with my worldly items. I just have to impress her with being myself. I lean in close to her and lower my voice so no one hears me. "You ready to make our great escape?"

She shivers, and fuck, if that doesn't make my dick twitch knowing I affect her. "I was ready the moment we arrived." I chuckle at her honesty and take her empty drink from her to place it on one of the tables. I grab her hand and we make our way back inside. We're stopped numerous times, but manage to get out of there twenty minutes later.

"Not so terrible, was it?" I ask after we get in the car and Sam drives us away.

She smiles sheepishly and looks down at her fidgeting hands. "No, not terrible at all."

A loud rumbling sound comes from her stomach and I look at her in surprise. "You barely ate anything. Want to grab a bite to eat?"

"I'm starving," she says, nodding. "If I remember correctly, there's a Culver's on the way home. I love their custard and it's been a long time. Do you mind if we do that?"

I was thinking more of a romantic candlelight dinner at one of the best restaurants downtown, but if that's what she wants, I'm more than happy to oblige. "What's Culver's?"

Her eyes go wide before her nose wrinkles in disgust. "You've never had Culver's before?"

"No," I chuckle at her horrified expression.

"You're a deprived child." She shakes her head at me, and then turns her attention to Sam. "Sam, do you know about Culver's?"

He looks at her through his rearview mirror and nods. "Yes, ma'am."

"Can you please take us through their drive-thru?"

"Not a problem."

"What's so great about Culver's?" I ask, my tone filled with curiosity. My mother didn't allow us to have fast food and the only time we had it was when our grandmother would take us to Navy Pier. My sister and I would stuff ourselves until we were sick and needed to throw up.

She thinks about it for a moment and then shrugs. "I guess just the artery-clogging goodness of everything being fried and then chasing it with a custard." She proceeds to tell me what her favorite items are on their menu and her description of everything starts to make me hungry.

We arrive about ten minutes later and Sam pulls through the drive-through. I roll down the window and am about to ask what she wants when she moves over to my side and leans out of the window. I don't hear a damn word she says since my attention is focused on her tight ass as she leans over me to place our order. My hand itches to spank her, then rub my hand around those sweet cheeks until I find my way under her dress. I fist my hand in her jacket that is next to me and try to mentally recount the alphabet in French. I close my eyes to regain my composure and when I open them, I see Sam looking at me from the rearview mirror with a smirk on his face.

"I hope you like everything on your burger," she says as she pushes away from the window and sits back on her side.

"I'm a vegetarian."

Her gaze whips back to mine in surprise and then narrows in suspicion. "Seriously?"

"Nope." I tease, hoping she didn't notice that I moved my jacket to cover my uncomfortable erection. She tries to pay with her money, but I block her from leaning over me again and hand the cashier my credit card.

"I'm just going to warn you that once in a while, I would like to pay for something," she tells me in annoyance when I hand her the food.

"I'll let you pay for our first non-contracted date. Deal?" I look at her sincerely, wanting her to see that I'm not joking about wanting more dates.

"Slick," she says before taking a French fry out of her bag and popping it into her mouth. "I'll think about it."

I smile in victory and then notice that we have three bags with three shakes. "Are you saving some food for a midnight snack?"

"No, I figured Sam might be hungry and ordered him some food." She inches her way closer to the front of the car and places the food in the passenger seat for him and hands over his shake, thanking him for taking us tonight. My heart grows with pride at watching her do another selfless act of kindness. I've never considered that Sam might not eat while he waits for me during events, and now I feel like a complete asshole for not thinking about that before.

"You're pretty amazing, Ariana Leighton," I tell her when she returns to her seat. I'm not hungry for food anymore; she's the one I want to devour right now.

"Why? Because I ordered Sam food? The poor guy has got to be hungry."

"Most people don't think like you do."

She just shrugs and focuses on unwrapping her burger. "I disagree. There's still lots of good people in this world." I watch her in fascination as she brings her burger to her mouth, her eyes closing as she takes a bite and a moan of satisfaction rumbles from her. I'm envious that food is making her this happy when I want it to be me making her moan with pleasure.

She opens up her eyes and notices my staring. She blushes

and nods her head toward my bag. "C'mon, I want to see if you like it."

I happily oblige, needing the distraction away from that delectable mouth of hers. I carefully unwrap my burger and take a bite. She laughs when my eyes widen in surprise at how unexpectedly delicious this burger is.

"Wow." She hands me a fried cheese curd. I moan with pleasure when the gooeyness of cheese explodes in my mouth. "Ok, you're right. This is pretty fucking incredible."

I'm rewarded with another laugh, and she proceeds to tell me how she discovered the wonderful world of Culver's. I get lost in listening to her tell some tales of her childhood and how her father would drive her out of their way in order to get Culver's when her mother would be working.

Our time together ends way too quickly, and my disappointment is profound when Sam stops the car in front of her house. She refuses to listen to me when I tell her not to grab up the garbage. I give up when I see she's determined to clean up and help her stuff as many empty items into the bags. I get out of the car to walk around to her side and open the door for her. I see her garbage cans are on the side of the house and I help her carry the bags to throw them away. Once that is done, I walk her to her front door.

"Thank you for a lovely evening," she says with a shy smile, and I love how awkward she sometimes gets. Her gaze keeps dropping to my mouth, teasing me with memories of how good she tasted. I can barely contain my hands at my sides, so I slowly inch my face closer to hers, my eyes never leaving hers. Her eyes widen, mouth slightly parted as her breathing gets heavy. I so badly wanted to claim those lips and I'm pretty confident that she would let me, but a promise is a promise. I move my head up and plant a kiss on her forehead instead.

"You just breached the contract." I can hear her smiling through her voice, and I chuckle that she thinks she's won.

"Does your father kiss you on your forehead?" I ask, looking into her eyes.

"Well, yeah," she answers in confusion.

"Then that can't be classified as sexual activity," I tell her with a mischievous grin. I take a step away from her and bow. "Thank you for tonight. I look forward to our next adventure together." I grab her hands and squeeze them, needing one more touch of her before I leave. "Sweet dreams, angel."

It pains me to walk away from her, but I do once I see her safely inside her house. I walk back to the car and get inside, the air is mixed with her perfume and Culver's, bringing a smile to my lips.

"Excuse me, sir?" Sam asks, breaking into my thoughts. I look up and meet his gaze in the rearview mirror.

"Yes, Sam?"

"I know it's none of my business who you date, but sir... she's a keeper."

I chuckle at how perceptive he is and am not surprised that he's fallen under her charm too. "I'm working on that, Sam." He nods back in agreement, and I sigh with satisfaction. Tonight was a great night and it's only going to get better from here.

Chapter Twelve

ARI

WARREN PICKS ME up in his own personal car from the store two days later for the next holiday party. I was expecting him to own some ridiculously expensive, flashy sports car but was surprised to see him drive up in an SUV. I look around the employee parking lot to see if anyone is watching me before hastily getting into his car.

"I think the coast is clear and your secret is still safe," he quips with a knowing smirk. No one has made any snide comments at work yet, which means Olivia has kept what she knows to herself.

"Seems so, but do we need to discuss the company holiday party this Sunday? Was that part of the five I signed up for?" We are one week away from Christmas and the store is open later than usual, so our holiday party is always on a Sunday at a restaurant after the store closes.

"It wasn't, but it can be if you want it to be."

I look at his handsome profile while he drives, contemplating how to respond. I need to be honest with myself. I've been enjoying every second I get with Warren, whether that's seeing him in person or talking to him on the phone. My pulse races at the sight of him and I love that it's his voice I hear right before I go to bed each night.

"I'm not sure yet. Don't know if I'm ready for even more scrutiny from the bitches of Bentley's."

"Who are the bitches of Bentley's?" he asks with a chuckle.

"Mostly all of the employees who work in the cosmetic and handbag departments." He raises an eyebrow at me, and I can tell he wants to hear more. "I truly believe they were all hired for their looks and then sales experience second. If you aren't aesthetically made up or look like you have money, then they aren't wasting their time on you."

"Sounds like they're just jealous of your beauty."

I shake my head at him since he doesn't understand that's not what they're thinking. "No, they hate me because I'm your personal shopper and they all dream about being Mrs. Warren Bentley."

He gives me a skeptical look before responding. "I mean, I know I'm irresistible, but that's pretty sad if that's truly their life mission." I roll my eyes at his cockiness, which only makes him laugh. "Sounds to me like that's even more reason for us to make our couple debut at the holiday party."

He gives me a wicked grin, and I can't help but stare at him. He's so hot and when he smiles at me like that, I feel like I'm in some sort of fantasyland that I wouldn't mind turning into a soft-core porno.

I'm probably going to be the one breaching this contract with sexual activity.

I shake my head to clear out my dirty thoughts and realize I haven't responded back to him. "Maybe you're right. It might be fun to show up together."

"I think kissing in front of them would make it even better."

"I'm sure you do," I laugh, enjoying how he encourages me to breach it. "So where are we going tonight that's so casual?"

When I saw on the schedule that jeans and warm clothes were recommended, my interest was piqued.

"Tonight's holiday party is being thrown by real estate mogul Patrick Laramie, and every year he rents out the McCormick Tribune Ice Rink for his holiday party."

"We're going ice skating?" I can't contain my excitement at the thought of going ice skating and it must show on my face, because he laughs at me.

"We sure are. Do you know how to ice skate?" I give him a disgusted look at even asking such a ridiculous question. "So that look means yes."

"It's been a long time since I've been. We used to go ice skating every Friday night when I was a kid. I always pretended I was an Olympic figure skater and daydreamed about winning a gold medal."

"Did you used to compete?"

"Nope, never took a lesson in my life. Just kept practicing until I got good at it."

"Good then you'll be holding me up tonight while we skate."

I give him a skeptical look, not believing what I just heard. "You don't know how to skate?"

"Not a lick."

"How can that be? You grew up here!"

"My parents wanted me to focus on playing lacrosse, so that's what I did," he says with a shrug.

I narrow my eyes and give him a naughty smirk. Of course Warren played lacrosse. This information doesn't surprise me in the least. "I can totally see you playing lacrosse. That's such a hot guy sport."

"You think I'm hot, huh?"

Damnit, Ari! You and your big mouth.

He looks so happy at this revelation that I shrug my shoulders and just own what I said. "Whatever, Mr. Cocky Pants. You know you're good-looking." I decide to change the subject to not inflate that ego of his anymore than it needs to be. "Were you any good at lacrosse?"

"I was very good," he says with such a smug expression that I can't help but giggle. "I actually was considering turning pro, but got injured in my junior year of college and that killed the dream of being a professional athlete."

"Oh wow, I'm sorry to hear that," I tell him with a frown. "Is that why you went into the family business?"

"I knew at a very young age that I would always be involved in the family business. I would've joined the company once my lacrosse career was over with, but since it never even began, I started working right out of college. My parents made me intern for free in every single department at Bentley Corporation first before I was even hired for a paying job."

"Really?" I'm impressed with this information because I just assumed he started in whatever position he wanted.

"It was important to them that I properly knew how to run the business since we have so many different divisions to the company."

"Do you have a division you prefer spending more time with than others?"

"The store is not my expertise. I like acquisitions and real estate. I feel I have a pretty good knack for that. But I make sure to surround myself with people who are the best in the industry and have our best interests at heart." He looks at me intently and I can tell an idea just came to his mind with the way his eyes light up. "I actually would like to get your opinion on a new division I want to start. Maybe we can chat about it while we skate since we're here."

He pulls the car into the parking garage and parks. We get out, and he grabs a large gift bag from the trunk.

"What's that?" I ask as he shuts the trunk and reaches for my hand. I happily take his as he starts to lead us out of the garage.

"Brand new toys. Patrick does a toy drive for the children's hospital."

I stop dead in my tracks, horrified that I came empty handed. "Oh my gosh, I didn't know! Warren, we must quickly go to the toy store so I can buy something."

"Sweetheart, all these toys and a very large check are from both of us. You're covered." He pulls at my hand, but I grab his wrist to pull him back.

"Warren, your money is *not* my money," I grit out through

my teeth, my jaw locked in frustration. "Please take me to the toy store."

With our hands still joined, he wraps our arms behind my back and pulls me against his chest. He brings his head down, his nose less than an inch away from mine. His breath is warm and smells like peppermints, and I gulp down the need to kiss him.

"Did your father ever spank you when you were a child?" he growls out in a low, husky voice. He's so close that I can see the gold flecks in his gorgeous aquamarine eyes. I slowly get lost in those eyes and don't answer him right away.

"Yes, but what does that have to do with anything?"

"Because if you continue to be argumentative with me, I will spank that fine ass of yours until you like it so much that you'll break our contract for it to become a sexual activity." I gasp at the desire that shocks me to my core from his words. I clench my insides, visions of him and I together sending tingles down my spine. If this is how I react to his verbal foreplay, then I have no doubt in my mind that sex with Warren will rock my entire world.

And there went my panties.

"Are you done being stubborn?" he whispers, his lips hovering over mine, teasing me with how soft they look. I stare at his bottom lip, craving to suck it between my teeth.

"For now," I whisper back and he chuckles. He moves our hands lower so his fingers lightly caress my ass. I bite my lip to keep my moan at bay because this is pure torture. I watch his lips slowly turn upward into a sensual smile. This man is becoming my kryptonite and soon I won't be able to resist him.

He kisses my forehead and steps back, bringing our hands forward. "C'mon, let's go ice skating." I nod my head and take in a shaky breath, slowly regaining my wits from another one of his trances. The crisp air feels good against my warm cheeks while we walk into Millennium Park.

We arrive at the outdoor rink and Warren introduces me to the Laramie's. Patrick can't contain his surprise when Warren calls me his girlfriend again. "Where did you two meet?" he asks and

I look up at Warren, an amused expression crossing my face.

Can't wait to hear this one.

"She's been my personal shopper at the store for the last four years and I didn't even know it. I went in to meet her in person for the first time and I've been under her spell ever since." I don't know why I was expecting him to lie, but his honest admission makes me very happy and I can't contain my smile.

We grab some hot chocolate and continue to mingle with guests who Warren knows. Everyone keeps saying they are surprised to see Warren tonight, which confuses me. Once we are finally alone to put on our skates, I ask him about it.

"I usually decline this invitation and just send in a check," he tells me while lacing up his skates.

"Why did you decide to attend this year?" I ask, distracted with my own skates.

"Because I knew tonight's party would be very date-like and thought you could use a little fun." My stomach does a somersault at how thoughtful he is. Come to think of it, he's been doing thoughtful things for me since the day he came to apologize.

When are you going to give him the chance he deserves?

When I stop being scared that he's going to break my heart.

I shake off my internal battle and finish tying my skates. I stand up and he follows suit, but not before he wobbles a bit. I grab his hand to steady him, a boyish look popping up on his face.

"You ready to show me your moves, angel?" he asks, my heart melting under his smile.

"I'm ready!"

This time he lets me lead him to the rink and with help from me and the wall, he manages to get on the ice and stands on his skates. It takes him a good ten minutes to get his big legs sorted out and I don't think I've ever laughed so hard in my life watching someone almost face plant so many times. Twice he almost took me down with him, but I managed to weasel my hand out of his death grip before he caused us both to get concussions.

I stick close to him, showing him how to move one foot at a time. Soon he starts to get the hang of it and ventures off on his own. I watch him move around the rink without me, a look of determination set on his face as he watches his feet while skating. He passes me by once, then gains his confidence to skate faster. After a couple of times around the rink, he tries to skate backward and to my annoyance, he nails it the first time.

It took me almost a year to confidently skate backward.

I scowl at him as he circles around me, irritated that he now looks as if he's been skating for years.

The man is good at everything he touches... sports, business, women.

"Spin with me." He startles me out of my thoughts and grabs my hands. We move toward the middle and start to spin in circles. His cheeks are rosy from the cold, his eyes shining with happiness. I stare at him, taking a mental picture of how he looks because I never want to forget this moment, of Warren looking so happy. The outside world starts to fade for me and all I see is him, smiling with the bright lights of downtown surrounding us and holiday music playing in the background.

Warren senses the shift in me and slows us down. He pulls me closer to him until I'm wrapped in his arms. I close my eyes and sigh, relishing in how good it feels to be in a man's arms.

His arms.

I slowly open my eyes back up to see him staring at me. His eyes are hooded with passion and I shiver, but not from the cold. The heat of his hunger courses through my veins and I don't want to resist him any longer.

"Warren," I say in a raspy voice. I gulp down my emotions and clear my throat from my nervousness. "I give you permission to kiss me."

He presses his forehead to mine, and I watch in anticipation as his lips turn into a smile and move closer to mine. "Is it just your lips I have permission to kiss? I just want to clarify because once I drink up your lips, I was hoping to kiss up and down the crook of your neck for a bit." His voice turns husky and I'm mesmerized by those full, soft lips. "And once I make my way down your throat, I would like to venture lower and kiss those perky nipples of yours." I sharply take in a breath, my nipples getting hard at the thought of being sucked on by him. "And when I'm done kissing them until they're hard, I was hoping to get permission to kiss down your body until—" He moves his lips across my cheek to my ear, nipping at my lobe. "—until I reach that delicious, wet pussy of yours that I want to kiss and suck for a very long time." I pant out the breath I was holding, clenching my walls so tightly that I might come from the images cascading through my mind. "Do I have your permission to kiss all of you, Ari?"

Yes, my whole body screams. *Get him inside you now!*

He brings his face back into my line of sight, and I feel his gloved hands holding my cheeks. He nuzzles his nose against mine and I grip his biceps hard in need. "Yes. Yes to all of it. *Please*, Warren." I have no shame in my begging.

He softly touches his lips to mine and I'm ready to go in for the kill when I hear someone screaming in the background, "Watch Out!"

And that's when another body plows into us, sending us crashing to the ice.

Chapter Thirteen

WARREN

I CAN'T CONTAIN the urgency I feel in needing to see Ariana again. It's been less than twenty-four hours and I've been on edge all day, counting down the minutes until it's time to pick her up for the next party. I've acted like a hormonal teenager all day—snappy and moody one minute, then happy with a stupid grin on my face the next.

"What's up with you today?" Delilah commented during lunch, giving me a look of disapproval. "Are you finally doing the nasty with Ariana? Because you're sure acting like you haven't."

"No, we haven't," I snap at her, not wanting to talk about my sex life with my own sister. "I'm just anxious to see her again," I admit, much to my sister's delight.

Ariana hurt her hip when we got knocked down at the party last night. I tried to convince her to let me take her to the emergency room, but she was adamant on not going. I took her home early, but not before we had a ten-minute make-out session in my car in front of her house. When she tried to lean closer into me, she knocked her injured hip into my center console, the pain quickly dousing her desire. After I helped her walk to her front door, I raced home and took a shower, coming hard in my hand with fantasies of her mouth around my cock.

I talked with her twice already today, and she kept reassuring me that she feels fine enough to attend tonight's party. I wonder what she would say if I pretend we're going to the party and just end up taking her on a real date. But tonight's affair is a more personal one, and my friends would be upset if I don't make an appearance.

Sam pulls up in front of her house, and I see she's already outside. "What are you doing out in the freezing cold?" I ask when I get out of the car and stride toward her. It snowed today and it would upset me if she slipped on any black ice.

"I needed to take the trash out. Your timing is perfect. Let me grab my purse and the white elephant gifts." The party's theme is ugly sweater with a white elephant gift exchange, and since I've never shopped for a white elephant gift before, I asked her to do it for us. In typical Ariana fashion, she refused the money I tried to give her for the gifts.

I wait for her by the front door and once she comes back out, make her hold on to my arm. She has a slight limp from last night's injury, and I feel guilty that she's not lying down in bed icing her hip. "Maybe we shouldn't go tonight. I don't want you to do permanent damage to your hip."

She rolls her eyes and shakes her head at me. "You're acting worse than my own mother. If I wasn't fine, I would tell you," she says with a scowl, making me chuckle. "Besides, I love ugly sweater parties and haven't been to one in a really long time."

"Fine, but if your hip starts to hurt, we're leaving," I warn her, to which she sticks her tongue out at me. A tongue I want to suck on so badly. I get her in the car and briefly adjust myself while walking to my side.

This is going to be a painful car ride.

"Where's Sam taking us to tonight?" she asks after I settle in, and Sam drives away from her house.

"We're going back up to the North Shore suburbs to my

friends Cal and Jenna's house."

"These are your personal friends and not business associates?" she asks, and I notice she bites her lip in nervousness.

"They're personal friends who recently have dabbled into my business." I study her to see if the names ring a bell. I can see the wheels turning and suddenly, her eyes widen.

"Cal as in Cal Harrington, whose wife's name happens to be Jenna?"

"That would be the one," I tell her with a smile, enjoying her freak out way too much.

"God, I wish you would've told me this before so I could be better mentally prepared."

"Prepared for what?"

"For her being rude to me in case she hated all the dresses I picked out for her." She looks like she's about to be sick to her stomach, and I grin at how she's worrying about other people again.

"That's what you're worried about?" She nods, looking at me as if she's about to kill me for withholding this information. "So you're not freaked out because you're going into the house of one of the most famous actors in the world?"

"No. Why would I care about that? He's a human being." Her demeanor changes and she groans, placing her hand over her eyes. "Oh god, please tell me this isn't going to be one of those infamous Hollywood orgy parties you hear rumors about?"

I throw my head back and laugh, because her expression says she believes it is. "I've laughed more in the last two weeks with you than I have in years," I tell her after I catch my breath. I grab her hand and bring it to my lips, wishing I rented out a limo for tonight to have some privacy instead of Sam's Escalade. "No, this is not a Hollywood orgy and even if it was, there's no way in hell I'm sharing you." She rewards me with a shy smile, and I need to figure out some way to get her alone tonight.

There's always their guest rooms.

"How do you personally know the Harrington's?" she asks, her question a welcome distraction from my perverted thoughts.

"Jenna used to live in my building. I became friends with

her and her ex-husband because I would see them at the gym or pool. But then I stopped seeing him with her and noticed a sadness in her eyes. One day she finally revealed they were no longer together. I always thought the guy was a douchebag, but maybe that was just how he acted with other men. I felt bad for her, like I needed to watch over her and make sure she was okay."

"Did you guys used to date?" she inquires, and I smile with satisfaction at the flash of jealousy I see in her eyes.

"We never dated. She's like another sister to me. I'm just glad she finally got a second chance at love."

"Do you really believe in love?" She shoots me a skeptical look before staring straight ahead at the road.

"My parents weren't the best role models of two people in love, but my grandparents were. I've seen it happen for my friends." I'm stalling, trying to figure out what to say, afraid I'll freak her the fuck out, but damnit, I want her to understand what I'm feeling. "I used to be skeptical, but the way I feel about you has changed my mind."

Her head snaps to me and I hold her gaze, willing for her to take me seriously. I've never fallen this fast or hard for anyone before, and Ariana needs to start realizing this is not a game for me. I've kept my part of the bargain about getting her mother into the Blackburn Institute. They have an appointment to go for a tour tomorrow. After tonight, there are only two more parties left for Ariana to fulfill her contractual obligation. I need more time alone with her, for her to realize I'm not the man she perceives me to be.

"So, um, we never got the chance to talk about the business idea you mentioned last night."

Disappointment fills my gut at her subject change, but I shouldn't expect miracles to happen overnight. I know she's fighting her feelings for me, but I also know that I'm slowly chipping away at that wall around her heart.

"Right, so Bentley Corporation hasn't formed a foundation yet. We've been generously donating for years, but I would like to set up a foundation that puts on various events to raise money for the non-profits in our community."

Her eyes brighten and she smiles, nodding in approval. "I think that's a wonderful idea and that you should move forward with it."

"I also think you should apply to be the foundation's director." She snorts, obviously thinking this is a joke. "Me? I have no experience working for a foundation."

"You had no experience being someone's personal shopper, but that didn't stop you from excelling at it."

"There is zero comparison between the two. I'm not suitable for the position."

"I disagree. You're energetic and passionate about doing right by others. You were going to be an environmental lawyer to help save the world and the people in it. That's the attitude that drives a foundation."

"Warren, I have no earthly idea how to even start a foundation, let alone run one."

"It's not like we're opening it up tomorrow. You will learn. Cal and Jenna have set one up, and I'm sure they would be happy to have you personally talk with their director." She continues shaking her head at me, and I decide to not push the subject. "I'm sorry. I didn't realize you wanted to continue on your journey as a personal shopper. If you aren't interested, we'll search for someone else when the time comes."

I pretend to watch Sam continue to drive us, sneaking a glance at her from my peripheral vision to see her lips have thinned. I bite my cheek to contain my smile. *Nerve struck.*

"I don't want to be a personal shopper for the rest of my life," she says softly after we sit in comfortable silence for a bit. "Honestly, it's only supposed to be a temporary gig until my mother..." She swallows down the rest of her sentence, and I can tell she's struggling with her emotions thinking of life after her mother is gone. I grab her hand and place it on my thigh, squeezing it for support.

"I understand. Let's not think about it." I bring her hand up to my lips and kiss it. She gives me a sad smile, and I feel like a complete asshole, again. I can't handle seeing her sad. Makes me feel helpless, and I fucking hate that feeling.

"It's probably something I need to start thinking about it," she admits, and I nod in response.

"Promise me you'll think about applying to the foundation?" She rolls her eyes but smiles at me. "I want to get hired because I *earned* the position and not because we're dating."

"We weren't dating when you were hired as my personal shopper," I point out. "And it's nice to see you're finally admitting we're dating." I dazzle her with a smile because her admission makes me so damn happy.

I chuckle as her cheeks turn a nice rosy shade of pink. I kiss her hand again, this time holding it to my lips for a little longer. Her gaze drops to my lips, watching as I lightly feather her hand with my kisses. "What am I going to do with you, Warren?" she whispers.

Love me, my heart screams, while my brain tells my heart to calm the fuck down. *What has this woman done to me?*

I'm brought out of my thoughts when I notice we've arrived at the Harrington's. A security guard is outside, and we hand Sam our identification so he can check us off his list. Once done, he returns our ID's and opens the gates for us. Sam drives up to the front of the house and gets out to open our doors. I help Ari out of the car and carry the gifts for her.

We let ourselves in and are greeted by a beautifully decorated house lit up with holiday decor and packed with people mingling and drinking. I grab Ariana's hand and lead us through the maze of people until I spot Cal. He sees us as we get closer and nods in greeting before bending down and whispering into Jenna's ear, who perks up and looks for us.

"You're finally here!" Jenna yells before giving me a hug. She stands back and before I can make proper introductions, she practically throws herself at Ari and wraps her in a hug so forceful that they almost topple over. "I'm so happy to meet you, Ari! Warren has told me so much about you."

I pat Cal's back in greeting and am about to tease Jenna about almost hurting my date when I notice Jenna's eyes. They're bright and wild looking, making me wonder how much she's already had to drink tonight. She looks beautiful, dressed up in a sexy elf costume that has such a low V-neck that I'm frankly shocked Cal's okay with her wearing this. He must have read my mind because while she's talking to Ari, he reaches over and adjusts the scarf that is wrapped around her neck so that it covers her cleavage. She swats his hand away while still talking, making me laugh at how she multitasks.

"Warren, I'm stealing Ariana to get her drink. Cal will take both of your coats and put them in the guest room. You can put the gifts by the tree and help yourself to a drink." We hand Cal our coats and before I can appreciate how hot Ari looks in a dress that has "Naughty" written across her chest, Jenna yanks her by the hand and they're off to the kitchen.

I wonder just how naughty my girl can really get.

"Jenna's in high holiday spirits," I joke with Cal, noting that I've never seen her so energetic.

"Yeah well, we have Robert to blame for that, and I'm going to kill the wanker."

"What do you mean?" Robert is Jenna's oldest friend and her personal assistant. He's treated like family in this house so Cal's words surprise me.

"He gave her a gummy."

"A gummy?"

"Yeah, you know, an edible. She's high as a fucking kite right now."

I shake my head in laughter because it all makes sense now. Jenna isn't a big drinker, so this explains her behavior.

"Has she been drinking too?"

"She sure has." We both watch as Jenna pours a big helping of punch for herself and Ariana in red solo cups.

"She's going to regret that in the morning," I tell Cal, who nods in agreement. "Have fun dealing with that one." I pat his back, and he shoots me a look of disgust.

"Let's go do our assigned tasks before the girls come back and Jenna gives me grief for not being a good host." Cal walks off to put our coats away while I put the gifts under the tree. I grab myself a beer from one of the drink stations before running into people I know. I make small talk, looking out for Ariana the whole time. When I don't see her and Jenna appear for another ten minutes, I excuse myself to search for them. I find them holed up in a corner of the dining room, giggling like schoolgirls.

"Ladies, what's so funny?" I ask as I approach, and I'm happy to see they're getting along so well.

"Oh, nothing. We're just trading Warren stories." Jenna gives Ari a wink, and the two exchange a knowing glance. I feel a hand on my back and turn to see another one of Jenna's best friends, Layla, coming over to greet me. I give her a hug and introduce her to Ari.

"I'm going to steal Jenna away from you guys so we can start the white elephant exchange. Make sure you grab a plate of food before joining us," Layla instructs, and the two women walk off.

"Jenna said she loved all of the dresses I picked out for her," Ariana says in relief. "Are the dresses for the same New Year's Eve masquerade ball that we're going to?"

"Yes, it's actually put on by her mother, who helps raise money for the Children's Hospital every year." I wrap my arm around Ari's waist and pull her into my side. I lean down closer to her ear and whisper, "I'm sorry that I left you alone with Jenna. Did she make you uncomfortable?"

"Oh no, I love her! She's so sweet," Ari says before taking a sip of her drink. I look inside the cup and notice the contents are almost gone already.

"What are you drinking?" I ask, wondering if Ari is a lightweight when it comes to alcohol.

"Some kind of punch Jenna gave me. It's delicious. Want to try?"

I decline the invitation and make a mental note to watch Ari closely.

"Let's go get some food and sit down for the exchange." I lead her to where the line for the food starts and we wait for our turn, chit-chatting with other people in line. We pile our plates up, refill our beverages, and find a spot by the tree.

For the next two hours, we laugh our asses off over the hideous presents that are exchanged. Ari received a naked garden gnome, and I got a scarf that has large breasts at either end. Ari has loosened up by the end of her second drink, and I love seeing her relaxed and having a good time.

When the exchange is over, the music gets cranked up, and Jenna steals Ariana from me once again to go dance with Layla on the make-shift dance floor located in the middle of the grand living room. I walk over to where Cal is and stand with him and Layla's husband, Chase.

"Where *is* Robert?" I ask, realizing that I haven't seen him all night.

"He's been passed out in one of the guest rooms since before the party. He took his gummy an hour before Jenna did and it seems he's a lightweight. I hope he wakes up with the worst hangover of his life."

I laugh at how serious Cal looks while saying that, knowing he means every word.

We watch the girls dance and I notice someone handing all of them shots. The three girls toast to each other and down them in one swoop. "I can't believe Jenna is still standing," I say to Cal while watching Ariana. I've never seen her smile and laugh this much and it's nice to see her having so much fun. This is exactly what she needed. I can tell she's buzzed from the alcohol, making me wonder if this shot is going to put her over the edge. I put my half-drunk beer down on the side table next to me and plan to switch to water for the remainder of the evening.

"Jenna is going to be incoherent shortly. I can see it in her eyes," Cal says, and I notice that he too is drinking water.

Chase draws my attention away from the girls when we start talking business, prompting me to ask him questions about his company's foundation. He provides me with some great information that I'm excited to share with Ariana. I glanced away from him to see the girls had left the dance floor and Cal left us as well. Chase and I split up to go find them.

My strategy is to find Cal because wherever he is, Jenna's usually with him. I finally find them in a hallway, making out like teenagers. He breaks their kiss and whispers something into Jenna's ear, making her give him a "you better fuck me now" look. She grabs his hand and they go through a door and shut it behind them.

I want Ariana to look at me like that, I realize, and go searching for her. I finally find her and Layla outside in the heated tent. Another drink is in her hand and I decide it's time for us to go home.

After much protesting from her and Layla, she finally agrees to leave. We go back inside to retrieve our jackets. I help Ari with her coat, grab our gifts and text Sam that we're walking out.

"Wait, we need to say goodbye to Jenna and Cal," Ari says, her words slurring while I help her keep her balance walking.

"They're indisposed right now," I tell her while holding her arm to lead her to the car.

"What do you mean?"

"They're fucking right now, Ari." I lean in closer to her so she's the only one who hears me. "Something I look forward to doing with you in the near future." She giggles and gives me a coy, sexy smile that instantly hardens my cock.

We get into the awaiting car and for the first fifteen minutes, Ari won't stop talking to Sam about how amazing Jenna is, what an amazing time she had and how amazing everyone was to her. Sam nods the whole time, chuckling at Ariana's overuse of the word amazing. Then she suddenly goes quiet and looks out the window. I glance away from her briefly to see our whereabouts and when I look back at her, she's sound asleep, her head tilted up against the headrest with her mouth wide open.

I take out my phone and try to read emails for the remainder of the drive, but her snoring and moaning keeps interrupting my thoughts. I gently pull her down so she can lay her head against my lap and I stare at her, caressing the hair from her face. Even in her slumber, Ariana is gorgeous. I wonder who she gets her looks from and my thoughts turn to our earlier conversation about her mother. Tomorrow is going to be a big day for them and I pray that Ari's hangover isn't too bad.

We pull up to her house and I reluctantly wake her up to help her get out of the car. I second guessed my decision to bring her home, but I didn't want to upset her parents. "Ari, should we go to my house?" I whisper as we reach the front door.

She shakes her head and squints at me, trying to focus on my face. "No, I'll be fine." I chuckle as she gives me a thumbs up before removing her arm from my shoulders.

"Sweet dreams, angel. Call me as soon as you wake up." I kiss her forehead and watch her slowly make her way inside. Once I hear the door lock, I walk back to the car.

So much for alone time with Ari, I muse, and plan another hot date in the shower with my hand.

Chapter Fourteen

Ari

ALCOHOL IS THE devil and I slurped up that Satan as if he was the only water left on this planet. No amount of ibuprofen is going to wash away my hangover headache. Thank goodness Warren took me home last night because I would've been mortified if he saw me puking like I did at two in the morning. I hugged the porcelain god for at least thirty minutes before picking myself up off the floor, brushing my teeth, and going back to sleep.

Since today is the day we tour the Blackburn Institute, I was smart enough to take the day off from work. To my surprise, so did my dad. It's nice having someone else fuss over my mom this morning since I wasn't in my usual good spirits.

"Someone might've had too much fun last night," my mom observes with a knowing smile when I drag myself out of bed and slouch into one of the kitchen chairs. She hands me a mug of coffee and toast with butter, knowing exactly what I need to calm my gurgling stomach.

"What kind of man lets his date get smashed the way you did?"

My dad looks at me over his morning newspaper, disapproval shining in his eyes.

"The kind who knows his date is an independent woman," I retort, not wanting to be lectured by my old fashioned father. "He didn't babysit me all night. We mingled, I met new people, they fed me drinks when he wasn't looking." Warren thinks I only had three drinks and a shot. What he didn't see was the other drinks I consumed with Jenna and Layla. It was nice being around women who didn't hate me for just being me, so I took advantage of it and had fun. "Warren offered to take me to his house so he could take care of me and not wake you guys up, but I told him no."

"Take care of you, huh? I know exactly what kind of 'taking care' he wanted to do to you," my dad mumbles, prompting my mom to smack him with her hand towel.

My dad would have an aneurysm if he knew the details of the contract I signed with Warren, so my mother and I agreed it would be our little secret until we were forced to tell him. All he knows is that Warren helped us get the appointment into The Blackburn Institute. He has no idea how much it costs to be there nor that Warren is footing the bill. He would view my contract with Warren as prostitution, even if we haven't had sex.

Yet.

I sigh and nibble on my toast while staring out the window and think about the sexy Mr. Bentley. Sex with Warren is inevitable because I'm done trying to control my lust for him. The man oozes sex no matter what he's wearing, whether he's smirking or scowling at you, and my defenses against him have diminished. I want him to do all the naughty things he whispered in my ear at the ice skating rink and then some. All I want for Christmas is Warren Bentley's dick inside of me and I'm pretty sure he would be more than happy to gift that to me.

The question still remains though if it would still be mine after the last party we attend on New Year's Eve.

I'm starting to believe it would.

"Time to get ready, Ari." My mother's voice cuts through my thoughts and I blush, thankful that she doesn't have a superhuman power of reading minds. My stomach gurgles again and I decide against eating my last piece of toast. I get up out of my chair and slowly ascend the stairs to my bedroom to get ready for the day.

We ARRIVE HOME hours later and I go straight to my room, needing a refuge to deal with my emotions. The Blackburn Institute surpassed my expectations with the kind of treatment my mother would receive and the facility was gorgeous, as if she would be living in a day spa. But it's still a harsh reality to what that place truly is – a last ditch effort at living with stage IV cancer. An extension of life if your body has not crossed the line of despair. After looking over my mother's medical records and evaluating her in person, they want her to start a three week stay and then one week at a time visits once a month for the next three months. My mother would've moved in today if we let her, but with Christmas and New Year's being right around the corner, we wanted to spend the holidays with her. So she agreed to check in on January 2nd. My father was too overwhelmed by it all to even ask how her treatment will be paid for and fortunately, the director never mentioned Warren's name.

I've been ignoring Warren's phone calls all morning, sending them straight to voicemail. I was going to call him this morning, but was pressed for time to get ready so I texted him instead telling him all was fine and I would talk later. Patience doesn't seem to be a virtue of his, because he's been calling me ever since we came home. I'm just not ready to talk about my feelings with regards to today. Yes, I'm eternally grateful to him for getting us in, but I'm also angry that we're even going through this. I just need time alone to calm down.

But Warren doesn't seem to want to give me that. My phone won't stop buzzing with incoming text messages from him.

Warren: Are you free to talk yet?
Warren: How did the appointment go?
Warren: Ari, are you okay?
Warren: Ari, your appointment was over two hours ago.

Where are you?

Warren: It's been four hours since my first text. I'm getting worried.

Warren: If you don't answer me right now, I'm coming over there.

I know he's not bluffing about making a surprise appearance, so with a huff of annoyance, I sit up in my bed and respond back to him. I text him that all is fine and talk later, but of course my phone rings ten seconds after hitting the send button.

"About fucking time, Ariana," he answers in an irritated voice. "Don't ever avoid me like that again."

Oh, no he didn't just answer the phone like that! "Did it ever occur to you that maybe I'm not okay from our visit today? That maybe I needed alone time to sort out my feelings and oh, I don't know, cry without an audience?" I yell at him, not taking his shit about not being at his beck and call.

"That's why I kept calling you, Ari. I knew today was going to be an emotional day and I wanted you to air it out to *me*." His voice softens and I hate hearing the concern in it. "You don't have to be going through this alone anymore."

"It's the only way I know how to get through this, Warren. It has been four years of being alone with this. You can't expect me to start telling you my every emotion right away when we've only just met."

"Why can't I?" he demands, bristling with temper.

"Because I'm not built that way, damnit!"

I expected him to come back with more demands, more stupid logic as to why I should be opening up to him and not bottling up everything inside of me, but instead the line goes silent and all I hear is a sigh.

"You're right, Ari, and I'm sorry for pushing you and acting like an insensitive asshole. It's just I remember what it was like when my mother was dying. I refused to talk to Delilah or my grandparents about it at first because I was a man, and I was brainwashed to believe that men shouldn't cry or show sadness. I remember how empty and isolated I felt because of my thought process and baby, I just don't want that for you."

I close my eyes and let the tears silently fall, praying he can't hear my ragged breaths. *This man is too good for me*, I think, covering my eyes with my free hand.

"Fuck the party tonight. Will you come over to my house and I can cook you dinner? We don't have to talk about today at all. Let's just talk about stupid shit, eat good food, and watch a bad movie that makes us laugh. Let's pretend life is normal for a night."

I forgot all about the fourth holiday party that was tonight. I'm in no condition to be going and am grateful that he sees that. "I would love that," I tell him because pretending to be normal sounds like heaven right now.

"I'll pick you up at six."

"I can drive my dad's car over."

"Ari, please let me pick you up so you don't have to worry or think about anything?" he pleads, his voice sounding like he's in pain due to the restraint he's having at saying please and not demanding that he pick me up.

"Okay," I say in resignation, too tired to even argue with him anymore. "See you at six."

HE BRINGS ME and my mother another bouquet of flowers when he arrives. I don't invite him in again, but my mother sneaks up behind me to greet him in person when I open the door. She gives him one of those tight, motherly hugs and thanks him for his kindness. Watching my mother hug Warren triggers my emotions and I bite the inside of my cheek to keep from crying. Warren senses my mood as soon as we get into his car and he drives us to his place in silence.

I've been intrigued about where he lives and knew from our conversation about Jenna being his former neighbor that he lived in a fancy high-rise condominium. What I wasn't expecting is that he lived in one of the most famous towers on Lake Shore Drive. Lake Point Tower is an iconic part of the city's skyline along Lake Shore Beach and one of the few buildings that has an unobstructed view of Lake Michigan.

"I can't believe this is where you live," I murmur when we get inside his condo, staring around in awe. The condo might be the same size as my house, but I was expecting someone like Warren to be living in a penthouse or one of those fancy four story brownstones. I walk over to the floor to ceiling windows and look at the shining lights of the pier. Even though it's dark outside, I can tell he has a wraparound view of the lake, probably one of the best views in the whole tower. "When I would go to Navy Pier as a child, I would always stare at this building and wonder what it would be like to live in a steel tower in the sky with a view of the lake."

His smile reaches his eyes, and I can tell he's happy with my response. "Let me give you a quick tour." It's a two-bedroom condo with an open floor plan and of course, it looks like it was decorated straight out of a high-end designer magazine. It has beautiful light fixtures and wide plank hardwood floors. The kitchen has shiny stainless-steel appliances and gorgeous marble countertops. His office is on one side of the condo with his master bedroom being on the opposite side. We walk into his bedroom and I'm surprised at how large it is. My gaze drifts over the built-in fireplace and lands on his California King bed. The air seems to change with an undercurrent of electricity, and I look up to see him watching me with hooded eyes.

Like always, Warren's sexiness steals my breath away. He's wearing a light gray mock-neck sweater with dark blue jeans and tan chukka boots. He again looks like he just stepped out of a catalog with his dark hair stylishly ruffled by his fingers. His smell is ingrained in the air and I have to physically stop myself from moaning out loud every time I inhale. I try to push my lustfulness aside and give him a tentative smile. He smiles politely back, gesturing his arm back in the direction of the living room.

"What's for dinner? It smells amazing," I ask as we walk out of his bedroom and back through his living room to the kitchen.

"Lasagna with garlic bread and salad."

"Sounds delicious. Where did you pick it up from?"

He gives me a smirk before popping the cork off a bottle of wine. "I made it."

I shoot him a skeptical look, trying to decide if he's serious or not. He notices my hesitation in responding and chuckles. "It's the one thing my mother taught me how to cook because it was always my favorite meal of hers."

My heart skips a beat at the idea of him making me one of his mother's meals. "I can't wait to try it," I tell him, genuinely excited he made us dinner.

He pours himself a glass of red wine and makes me a vodka tonic with lime. I stare at the glass skeptically after he puts it in front of me. "Yeah, I don't know if drinking that is such a good idea."

"Just take a couple of sips to calm your nerves and we can throw the rest away."

I do as he says before putting the drink down to address the elephant in the room. "So about that. I'm sorry for earlier."

"You have nothing to apologize for, Ariana, and we don't have to talk about it." He gives me a stern look while tossing the salad together, causing me to bite my lip at the dirty thoughts that are blazing in my mind about him and tossing other kinds of salad.

Does he like tossing salad?

Would I like getting my salad tossed?

What in the hell is wrong with me to be thinking about this?

I shake my head to clear it and notice he's looking at me, a concerned smile on his face. "You okay over there?"

"Not really," I say in all honesty. I take a sip of my drink and grimace, deciding against drinking any alcohol this evening. "Blackburn Institute was wonderful. The facility is beautiful and everyone seems nice."

"Your mother will be well taken care of during her stay. Some patients joke that they never want to leave."

"I can see that. It looks like a high-end day spa. She'll start her treatment after the new year." I look down at my fidgeting hands and swallow the lump of emotions that always seems to well up inside of me when talking about my mother. "It's going to feel weird not having her around for three weeks," I think out loud to him. "I don't think my dad is going to handle it too well. It'll be a reminder to him of what the future is bringing."

Warren grabs plates and bowls from one of his cupboards and brings them over to where I'm sitting. "Your father will probably immerse himself into work. That's what we do when we're stressed or upset. Anything to escape reality."

He's probably right because even with her home now, my dad's barely around. "Maybe I should do the same."

"Maybe we should take a vacation."

He said the word "we" and my stomach does a belly flop. There's nothing more I would love to do than to live out my fantasies of Warren and me on a tropical beach somewhere on a remote island. Unfortunately, reality sucks a big one because that won't be happening anytime soon. "I don't have any more vacation time left. I used all of my sick and vacation days for her chemotherapy appointments."

He frowns at that, but doesn't say anything and continues setting up for dinner. I wish there was a way to repay him for helping my mother out, but there isn't and I just need to accept that.

"Thank you again, Warren. For everything," I softly say, not able to look him in the eye. I feel him grab my chin between his fingers, lifting my head up so I have no choice but to look at him.

"When are you going to realize that I'll do anything for you?"

I inhale sharply, my mouth parting at how his words decimate my heart. Before I can respond, he swiftly claims my lips in a kiss that scorches my panties. His lips are firm and demanding and I moan in happiness when his tongue clashes with mine. I stand up and wrap my arms around him, plastering myself to that rock hard body of his. I'm ready to start taking articles of clothing off when the oven timer chimes, rudely interrupting our make-out session.

He removes his lips and places his forehead against mine, both of us trying to get our breathing under control. "I better take the lasagna out before it burns," he says reluctantly before releasing me and going toward the oven. My body silently protests as I watch him walk away, already missing his warmth and touch. I decide to busy my brain and my hands by helping him.

Dinner turns out surprisingly delicious and the conversation flowed easily between us. He told me about the latest commercial real estate Bentley Corporation just purchased, his conversation with Chase Wilson the other night regarding starting a foundation, and how his grandmother is enjoying her vacation in Australia.

"What are you doing for Christmas?" I ask him while I load our dirty dishes into the dishwasher and he puts pre-made cookie dough on a tin pan.

"Since Grandmother isn't around, Christmas will be at my dad's house." He puts the pan in the oven and closes the door.

"You don't sound too enthusiastic about it."

I get the sense that Warren is not close with his father. He barely ever mentions him when talking about his family.

"It's always awkward spending time with my father and his other family. My stepmother is only five years older than me and made a pass at me first. Once she saw I wasn't interested, she zeroed in on my father who took the bait. My half-brothers are spoiled, arrogant brats and with me being eighteen years their senior, it's hard to have anything in common with them right now."

I shoot him a look of pity because it doesn't sound like Christmas is going to be relaxing for him whatsoever. "Will Delilah be there too?"

"Yes, but she's always in bitch mode and just can't let it go that he has a new family that he's more interested in than us. Honestly, if he wasn't still on our board, I think we both would stop talking to him."

"So why do you bother even going if you don't want to be around them?" I inquire, not understanding how someone like Warren who does whatever the hell he wants to do still feels obligated to see his father for Christmas.

"Because I know my mother would want me to and for some reason, I still like doing things that would make her happy, even in memoriam."

This speaks to my soul since not only would I feel the same

way, but it shows more of Warren's vulnerable side to me. His outside demeanor might look beautifully arrogant and cocky, but Warren is all heart to those that he loves.

"Do you think that sounds crazy?" He looks over at me with a boyish grin while taking the finished cookies out of the oven and my heart melts at how vulnerable he looks.

"No, it makes perfect sense to me." I finish loading the dishwasher, close it up and move to stand next to him.

"Have you made a decision about the company holiday party?" he asks while putting the hot cookies on a plate.

"I work all day Sunday, so honestly, I'd rather go home and spend time with my mom." My decision to skip the holiday truly has nothing to do with Warren. I skipped the party last year as well, so it's not like I'm missing some huge event. "Are you okay with that?" I ask, hoping he's not upset if I choose not to go.

"I have no problems with that." He puts the pan in the sink and pushes the plate of cookies toward me. "Hope you like gooey chocolate chip cookies."

He hands me a cookie and I take a bite. I close my eyes and moan in happiness as liquid chocolate explodes in my mouth. "These are amazing," I tell him in between bites of the cookie.

He stares at my lips and I dart out my tongue to grab any remnants of chocolate on them. "You missed a spot." He slowly rubs the pad of his thumb over my lips and then brings it to his mouth and sucks on it. I gulp down the rest of my cookie as I feel something else explode in my panties.

"Delicious," he whispers huskily. He grabs my hand that was holding the cookie and continues sucking and licking off all the remaining chocolate that was on them. Every touch of his tongue is like shots of flames to my core.

Holy shit, I'm in trouble.

"I want more," he demands, before cupping my cheeks in his hand and crushing his lips to mine. I thrust my hands in his hair, open my mouth for him and groan at how delicious he tastes. He thrusts his tongue in and out, over and over again, making me delirious as my need for him intensifies. I wrap my arms around his neck as he kisses me deeper and hoists me up onto the kitchen island. I spread my legs and he nestles in between them, looking into my eyes with a sexy smile that is conquering my heart.

"You're the only dessert I want tonight."

He claims my lips again and in my tidal wave of desire, I feel his hands slide under the hem of my tunic, his fingertips sending tingles down my spine. I moan into his mouth as his kisses become rough and demanding. He breaks away to lift my shirt over my head and then pulls me back to him, drugging me yet again with his lips. He starts kissing down the side of my neck while his hands reach behind me to unhook my bra. He gets it on the first try, brings the straps down my arms and throws the bra to the floor.

"You're so fucking beautiful, Ari." He feathers kisses down my sternum while he leans down and cups one of my breasts in the palm of his hands. I wrap my legs around him and bring him tighter against me, my inner walls clenching at the need of him. He rubs the pad of his thumb against the bud of my nipple, the sensation a mixture of pleasure and pain. I break our kiss and pant out his name, arching my back at how amazing he feels. I look at him as he watches my nipple harden under his touch. His gaze comes back up to mine, his bright blue eyes blazing with passion.

"I'm going to kiss every inch of this gorgeous body of yours." I gasp as I watch him take my nipple into his mouth and he growls. He attacks my nipple, gently at first and then becomes rougher to the point that I'm rubbing myself up against him, ready to come. Knowing that I'm close, he releases my nipple and teases me more with his kisses up and down my sternum until he attacks my other breast with the same hunger.

"*Warren*," I whimper, grasping his head to bring his lips back to mine. He continues kissing me while his hands slide down my stomach to the top of my leggings. His fingers make their way into the waistband and start to slide down my hips.

"Lay back," he demands and gently grasps my biceps to lay me down. The marble is cold against my back, but it doesn't cool down my raging desire for him. He pulls me closer to the edge of the island and yanks my leggings and thong down my thighs and past my calves and feet to the floor.

"*Fuck...*" he breathes before kissing the inside of my right thigh. He stops short of touching my clit and moves to the other thigh. I'm thrashing around, thrusting myself in his face, needing to feel his tongue on me. He spreads my legs wider and I feel the tip of his nose nestle against my soaking wet clit.

"You smell like heaven," he groans out before flicking his tongue against my clit. I cry out in ecstasy as he slowly pushes two fingers inside of me. His tongue starts sucking on my bud while his fingers move in and out of me. Licking, sucking, pumping...his tongue and fingers continue their assault on me and go faster and faster. He eats me out as if I'm his last meal for eternity. I grip his head and start rocking against him, my orgasm building fast and furious.

"Please Warren," I moan, my pussy throbbing against his fingers, ready to explode. He starts moving his fingers in a circle, then glides them in and out, exactly how I imagine his cock would feel. He grabs my hips harder and pushes his head into me deeper, his tongue becoming rough as he continues to lap me up.

"That's it, come for me baby," he growls against me as he feels my walls grip his fingers tighter. He places both of his hands under my ass and devours me.

"Oh my god, Warren...*yes!*" I scream, the tremors inside of me finally exploding. I tighten my thighs around his head as I ride out my orgasm against his fingers and tongue. I arch my back and grip him as hard as I can before letting go and going limp like a rag doll.

I can't seem to catch my breath as I throw my arm across my eyes, twitching from the remnants of my orgasm. I feel him kissing up my stomach, nuzzling his nose into my belly button. I've never had such an intense reaction to oral sex like that before in my life. Warren laces his hands through mine and slowly brings me up and holds me in his arms until I've stopped shaking. He holds my face and kisses me softly before looking into my eyes and taking a deep breath.

"Goddamn, that was fucking hot." He kisses me one more time before hoisting me up and carrying me over to the couch. He lays me down, grabs the blanket off the back of the couch, and drapes it over me.

I can see his erection straining against his pants and I reach for him, but he grabs my hand and squeezes it. "Tonight's about you, baby. I'll be a selfish prick next time," he gives me a sexy wink, causing my core to clench and I wonder when the next time will be.

Chapter Fifteen

ARI

NEXT TIME DIDN'T happen that evening, with me falling asleep on the couch while we watched a movie. Warren gently woke me up and drove me home, where I crashed and had even more wet dreams of him. Work consumed both of our schedules during the next couple of days. We didn't get to see each other in person like I hoped we would, but we talked on the phone multiple times a day. Even though I heard his voice every day, I physically missed seeing him.

Christmas Day arrived and my mother surprised me and my dad with handmade blankets. I didn't even know my mother could knit and she apparently had been keeping it a secret from us. I teared up when I took the blanket out of its box, grateful that I'll have another item that she made for me to remember her by.

We kept up with our traditions of ordering Chinese food for dinner and watching holiday themed movies. We were about to start another movie when my phone alerted me of a text message. I looked down to see it's from Warren, who was supposed to be at his father's house.

Warren: Can I steal you for just a few minutes? I'm outside and wanted to wish you a Merry Christmas in person.

My heart starts hammering in excitement at getting to see him, and I tell my parents to start the movie without me.

"Where are you going?" my mother asks and there's no way I can get out of not telling them.

"Warren's outside. I'll only be a couple of minutes," I say while putting my winter coat on and sliding my feet into my shoes.

"Wait, I have a present for him." My mother gets out of her chair and walks into her room. She emerges with a small, wrapped present. "I made him a scarf."

I look at her in surprise, tears springing to my eyes at her thoughtfulness. "That's sweet of you, Mom."

"It's the least I can do," she says with a small smile. "You know, one day it would be nice if you invited him over."

I give her a smirk, knowing exactly what she's implying. "Maybe one day I will."

"Maybe next year, since that will be in a week." I laugh at her persistence and grab the present from her to go outside to meet him.

He's leaning against his car in a black puffer jacket, blue jeans and boots. He pushes off and strides toward me with a bag in his hand and a shit-eating grin plastered on his face. I can't contain my own smile, excited that I get to see him.

"Hello beautiful." He engulfs me in his arms and starts kissing me as if we aren't standing outside of my parents' house, who are probably watching us from the window. But I don't care if they are watching. I kiss him back with the same raw of hunger he kisses me with.

"Why aren't you at your dad's house?" I ask after we break our kiss, struggling to catch my breath.

"Been there, done that. We ate an early dinner and I left right after presents were opened. Besides, I wanted to give you your present." He hands me the gift bag with a smile.

"Warren, I wish you wouldn't do that," I groan because I

don't have a present for him. We didn't talk about exchanging gifts and I hate not being prepared. "My mom's a better person than I am because she has this gift for you," I tell him, handing him her gift. "But I'm sorry, I don't have anything for you. I didn't know we were doing presents."

"You're the only present I want," he murmurs before searing me with another kiss. He abruptly pulls back and smiles like a little boy bursting with excitement at a present. He rips off the wrapping from my mom's gift and reveals a beautiful navy knitted scarf. "Did your mom make this?" he asks, admiring the scarf in appreciation before wrapping it around his neck.

"She did," I say with pride, noticing that the color of the scarf makes the blue in his eyes shine even brighter.

"It's wonderful. I needed a new scarf." He tucks the ends of it into his coat and again, the man looks ready for a photo shoot. He nods his head toward the gift bag I'm holding and says, "C'mon, open your present. I want to see if I'm getting as good as you are with picking out gifts."

I bite my lip and look at him, feeling like a nervous nelly while taking the wrapped gift out of the bag. I recognize the wrapping paper to be from Bentley's and my heart starts hammering faster in my chest. I tear apart the paper and open the box, gasping in shock at what's inside. It's the same floral scarf that I loved and picked out for his grandmother, but it's a different color. Hers was light pink with pastel colors whereas this one is baby blue with the florals in gemstone colors. I've never seen this version of the scarf and I love it even more than the other one.

"How did you know?" I whisper, looking at him in awe.

"When you were showing me the scarf for my grandmother, you had this look on your face like you didn't want to give it up. I could tell that you loved it and I thought how cool it would be if my favorite girls each had one from me. I got Delilah one as well, but in her own special color."

"It's exquisite," I breathe out, loving the thoughtfulness behind it. "I've never seen this color before. We don't carry this in the store. How did you find it?"

"Olivia helped me," he says with a wicked glint to his eye.

I reach up on my tippy-toes and kiss that sexy smirk. "I love it, Warren. Thank you."

"You better think of me when you wear it," he demands before planting another kiss on my lips.

"You know I will." I bury my face in his chest and wrap my arms tightly around his waist. His smell permeates my senses and I don't want to let him go.

"Merry Christmas, angel," he whispers against the top of my head. I lift up my face from his chest to give him one last kiss before he leaves.

"Merry Christmas, Warren."

"Go get inside before you freeze," he tells me and I nod my head, letting my arms drop from around his waist in disappointment. I give him a sad smile and turn around.

Every step feels wrong, my body already missing his warmth, his touch. *Let him in*, my heart is screaming at me and I suddenly stop before reaching my front door and turn back around.

"Do you want to come inside?" I say rapidly before I change my mind. He steps closer, his eyes narrowed and a skeptical smile playing on his face. I swallow the lump in my throat and tell him, "We aren't doing much, just about to watch *Home Alone*, which I know, silly movie to watch, but I picked it out." I continue rambling, my brain mentally telling me to shut the hell up and let him answer. "I completely understand if you don't want to though." I exhale out the last words and hold my breath, waiting for his answer.

Gah, what am I doing?

You're letting him in.

He walks slowly up to me and cups my face in his hands. He tortures me with a chaste kiss to my forehead before answering. "There's nowhere else I rather be than with you."

I nod in happiness because he's robbed me of my thoughts once again. I grab his hand, take a deep breath and walk him inside my house.

THE DAYS LEADING up to the New Year's Eve masquerade ball flew by in a haze. Something shifted inside of me watching Warren with my family on Christmas Day. He made himself right at home and his presence in my living room felt as if he'd been part of the family forever. He was astute to pick up on that my father didn't know about our contract by the kind of questions my dad was asking him. Fortunately, Warren winked at me when he saw my concern and eased my anxiety about not saying anything.

This time of year is always crazy for me at work, but physically seeing Warren became a priority. He met me every day for lunch at our coffee shop so that we could get some time together. Once my lunch hour was up, he always walked me back to work, but not before leaving me hot and horny with a make-out session against one of the walls behind the building.

"Spend the night with me after the party?" he asked yesterday after another intense make-out session where I literally almost came from his rough, hot kisses.

I stared into his eyes and without hesitation, told him yes.

Now today is the day and my emotions are a rollercoaster ride. I'm excited and anxious to be with him, but nervous at the same time. Olivia notices the shift in my emotions and tries to calm me down.

"I know you picked out a dress already for tonight, but when Warren came by to shop for your Christmas gift, he actually found a dress that he would rather you wear instead."

"You showed him my dress?" I ask in annoyance, because I wanted everything to be a surprise. Now that Olivia has helped Warren once, she thinks they're besties.

"Of course *not*," she says in irritation, rolling her eyes. "I told him that it was top secret and he would probably rip it off of you as soon as he saw you in it, but he still went perusing into the dress department and came back with another dress. He insists you wear it."

"Of course he does because Warren always gets his way." The man is so bossy and I can't lie – it's sexy as sin.

"Got to say, the man has impeccable taste. Even though I love what you picked out for yourself, the dress he wants you to wear blows it out of the water."

"Really?" For Olivia to say that means the dress must be stunning. "Let me see it."

"Nope, you aren't allowed to yet. Not until your hair and make-up stylists have arrived and start getting you ready."

"What hair and make-up stylists?" I ask in confusion. "I never made an appointment with any."

"But your boyfriend did," she sings out, an evil grin appearing on her face as she watches my mouth drop open in shock. "They'll be here at five to get you ready for the ball, Cinderella." She grabs my hands, pulls me out of my chair and starts jumping around like a lunatic, squealing in excitement. All I can do is laugh at her because I'm still in shock at his generosity.

"Is this real life?" I say out loud, because I'm starting to feel like it's a dream. That nagging voice inside my head of Warren being too good for me appears and I quickly kick that out of my brain.

"By the way, I hate you and am happy for you all at the same time. Does Warren have any good-looking, rich cousins that you can hook this girl up with?" I giggle at her and shrug, not really knowing that answer.

"We'll find you your Prince Charming one day, Liv. You just might have to go through a lot of frogs to find him," I tell her and give her a hug. "Thank you so much for being such an incredible friend and supporting me."

"Oh please." She waves her hand at me like it's no big deal, but it is to me. I barely have any friends anymore and to be able to count on her means a lot. "I should be thanking you for putting up with my crazy ass." We laugh at the truth in her statement and hug it out before getting ready for our next client appointment.

Back-to-back appointments made the day speed by and five o'clock arrived faster than I was ready for. Olivia escorted the stylists to our largest private dressing room that she reserved for us to use. I learned from the stylist that they just left Jenna Harrington's house and I know I'm in the best hands in the business. They effortlessly worked at the same time on me and an hour later, I'm in awe of the girl in the mirror. Even I'll admit that I look beautiful and am happy to see that the make-up artist didn't drastically alter my appearance. The hair stylist blew out my hair, adding volume to my crown and loose waves, making it cascade down my back.

"Ready for your dress?" Olivia asks and without waiting for me to respond, starts unzipping the large garment bag. My eyes widen as she takes out a white floor length off-the-shoulder organza ball gown with cap sleeves. The dress is a mix of sultry sexiness and graceful elegance. I absolutely love it more than the dress I picked out for myself.

"It's white," I murmur while tracing my fingers over the delicate fabric. I don't want people to think it looks like a wedding dress.

"Who the hell cares about that?" Olivia looks at me as if I'm crazy. "It's perfect. Besides, we're pairing it with black satin gloves and these shoes." The shoes she pulls out are a gorgeous pair of black satin heels with crystal embellishments on the front.

"Wow," is all I can muster out. "I can't believe he did all of this."

"The clock is ticking. Lift your mouth up off the floor and let's get this baby on!" Olivia helps me carefully get the dress on and zips it up in the back for me. Once the dress and gloves are on, Olivia hands me an exquisite black lace masquerade mask encrusted with black rhinestones. Before she can help me with the mask, there's a knock on our door.

"Who is it?" Olivia asks and opens the door a crack, blocking me from seeing who it is. I hear Warren's deep voice and the butterflies in my stomach start to act up. I can't wait to see how handsome he looks in his tuxedo.

"You can't see her yet, it's bad luck!" I hear Olivia tell him and I start to laugh because she's really crazy.

"Liv, it's not our wedding day. Let him in!"

She rolls her eyes at me but proceeds to open the door for him. Warren takes two steps in and stops, his eyes slowly drinking me in from head to toe. He looks devastatingly handsome in his black tuxedo, and I can't believe how lucky I am to call him mine.

That's right, Ari, he's yours. Now start acting like it.

I nod at myself and walk toward him. His gaze is heated with passion, sending shivers down my spine knowing what's to come tonight.

"You take my breath away, Ariana Leighton." He softly touches my lips with his and I can tell he's refraining himself from kissing me deeper.

"Don't ruin her make-up, lover boy. That's for later." Olivia reminds him, causing Warren to chuckle against my lips.

He pulls back from me and gives Olivia a wink. "Yes, ma'am," he salutes her, and she starts fanning herself with a piece of paper. She hands him a faux-fur black shawl that he slips up my arms onto my shoulders.

"Thank you, Warren. For everything." I tell him, hoping he sees in my eyes that I mean so much more than just for today.

He grabs my gloved hand and kisses the top of it. "Ready to go, angel?" He takes my overnight bag from Olivia and offers me his other arm. I grab my mask and clutch before hugging Olivia and whispering thank you in her ear before we head out.

We make our way downstairs to the employee parking lot and I can feel the eyes of the bitches of Bentley burning through my skin as we glide past them. I look at Warren and smile when he winks at me. Let these women gossip and say nasty things about me. I honestly don't care anymore. Warren knows I want him for him and that's all that matters.

Sam is waiting for us when we get outside and opens the door for us. Warren helps me into the car and shuts the door. Once he's inside, Sam takes us to our destination.

"Why are you sitting so far away from me?" I ask Warren, noticing that he's closer to his door than he is to me.

"I'm not in control of myself right now, Ariana. All I want to do is throw up your dress and fuck you in the back of this limousine." I clench my thighs together with longing and muffle my moan at the images his words bring to mind. "I'm just warning you now, we're not staying long tonight."

I giggle and nod in agreement, completely compliant with

his decision. The nice thing about tonight's event is that it's in the grand ballroom at Navy Pier, which is right next to Warren's condominium.

It takes us less than ten minutes to get to Navy Pier. Sam pulls up to the front and Warren instructs him to drop off my overnight bag at the house and that he's dismissed for the night. We put our masks over our eyes and exit the car. We walk up to the event coordinator and show her our identification. Once she approves us, we walk into the building.

The theme of the masquerade ball is one of an enchanted garden. The front entrance has a gorgeous archway of flowers welcoming us in. We make our way inside the ballroom and even more whimsical flower arrangements appear as centerpieces on each table. A stage with a dance floor is toward the rear of the room and multiple bars are set up in each corner.

I smile politely at the people who say hello to Warren but it isn't until I see Jenna and Cal that I let my guard down and relax a bit.

"Ari, you look stunning," Jenna says to me as she greets us. She leans closer to my ear and whispers, "Warren looks like he's ready to eat you." I blush ten shades of red as the memory of him eating me out on his kitchen island comes to mind. Jenna sees my embarrassed look and throws her head back in laughter.

"I think Cal is looking at you in the exact same fashion." Cal's eyes are hooded as he briefly nods at me and returns his gaze to his wife. I can't blame him as Jenna looks even more beautiful than usual tonight. She's wearing a shimmering gold V-neck long-sleeve gown that hugs all of her curves with a high slit all the way up her left thigh and a matching mask covering her face. Her long caramel hair is down like mine and in waves.

She notices me staring at the slit up her leg and rolls her eyes. "Cal makes it mandatory that all of my gowns must have this ridiculous slit in them." She leans in closer so only I can hear her. "Says it's for him to have easier access." She gives me a wink and we laugh at how demanding these men are.

More people come to our group and Jenna introduces me to her parents and her assistant Robert, who I didn't get to meet at her party. I notice Warren hands Jenna's mother a check and with the way she screamed in delight once she opened it, I'm assuming it was a very large donation to the children's hospital. I feel tears start to well up and as if sensing my emotions, Warren looks over at me and gives me one of his heart-melting smiles. I so unfairly judged this man and I say a private thank you to God for bringing him into my life.

We collectively as a group make our way to the bar and order drinks. Warren holds my hand as we walk around the ballroom to our designated table. We don't sit down yet and all of us stand outside of our chairs and continue talking.

I'm chatting with Jenna about my mother when I see her eyes widen at something over my shoulder. "Don't turn around, but Warren's ex-fiancée is coming toward us." My eyes widen and it takes every ounce of my self-control not to look. I have no idea what she looks like and I'm dreading to see how gorgeous she probably will be.

I turn to look over at Warren and see her hand snake up his arm and grab his shoulder. He turns toward her and I see a stunning woman with long, straight blonde hair in a dress that leaves little to the imagination. She's tall and slender and seeing her standing next to Warren, I can admit they once made a striking looking couple.

Warren knocks her hand off his shoulder and slides his hand around my waist, pulling me into him. He nods at his ex in coldness, his eyes showing disdain and boredom at having to waste his time in greeting her. "Hello Tamara. This is my girlfriend, Ariana. Ari, this is Tamara Dontell."

She looks down her nose at me as I offer her my hand to shake. "Nice to meet you." She shakes my hand but barely grips it. I nod at her, not even wanting to be fake by saying "likewise".

She introduces her husband, an older gentleman who barely acknowledges us and focuses his attention on Cal.

"So how long have you two been dating? Last time I checked you were dating some model, Warren."

"I see what you're trying to do Tamara and it won't work. My personal life is none of your business."

"Like I care about your life," she hisses at him before setting her sights on me. "Let me give you a little bit of advice on this one, sweetheart. He prefers work over his women."

"Maybe he was just bored with what was waiting for him at home," I shrug and give her a once over before staring her down. I refuse to let her think she can intimidate me or talk that way about Warren. She snorts in disgust, whips around and walks away from us.

"Bravo, Ari," Jenna leans over and whispers in my ear. My heart is pounding in anger at what a despicable human being that woman is.

"Excuse us, Jenna, but we're going to dance." Warren drops his arm and laces his fingers through mine to lead me to the dance floor. Once there, he hauls me against his chest and I wrap my arms around his neck.

"I'm sorry if Tamara upset you, angel," he says into my ear so I can hear him over the band playing.

"It's not your fault. What she said about you was unfair."

"Maybe, but you defending me made me hard as fuck." He presses me into his erection and I groan at how good he feels. "We're going to eat dinner and as soon as they take our plates away, we're leaving,"

"Do we have to eat dinner?" I ask with hope that he says no.

At my question, he rewards me with a wicked grin and a husky chuckle. "You're going to need every ounce of energy in that body of yours for what I have planned for you tonight."

Holy. Shit.

I bite my lip and look at him in longing, praying that we're called to our seats soon to start dinner.

Of course that doesn't happen and it's another forty-five minutes until Jenna's mother gets on the microphone to ask us to take our seats. With three hundred people at this event, dinner drags on and we don't finish eating for another two hours. But true to his word, as soon as Warren sees that I'm finished eating, he announces our departure.

Jenna's mother protests that we still have dessert and the silent auction to get through, but Jenna silences her with the reminder that Warren has already made a sizable donation. We say our goodbyes and hastily leave the party.

I was boiling inside the ballroom and not because the heater was turned up. Warren's lustful stares turned up my body heat so much that I welcomed the cold air as soon as we got outside.

"What are you doing?" he asks when he sees me take off my shoes.

"Run with me." I grab his hand and we start running to his building, laughing like teenagers along the way.

We get inside the building and he attacks me in the elevator, his tongue hot and wet when it runs along my bottom lip and into my mouth. He presses me against the wall, and I hold onto the rail for dear life as he kisses down my neck to my sternum.

We arrive at his floor and as soon as the elevator doors open, he grabs my hand and tugs me toward his apartment. I run to keep up with his long strides and once we're at his door, he punches his number into the keypad and opens the door for me. I walk past him, throw my shoes down and start taking off articles of clothing as I stride straight for his bedroom. First the shawl and then gloves hit the ground the moment I make it inside his room. I turn around right before I reach his bed and we stare at each as he advances toward me.

Our chests heaving and our eyes lock on each other's lips. Once he's only inches away from me, he places his hands on my hips, leans down, and claims my mouth. Softly at first, but soon the kiss becomes hot and he slips his tongue past my lips, making me moan as I grip his head and bring him closer to me. The kiss starts to become wildly out of control, and I feel his hands slide down my back, grab my ass and crush my pelvis to his so I can feel his erection.

While he lights my core on fire with his kisses, he reaches for the zipper on the back of my dress and brings it down. I feel the fabric loosen and I let go to bring the cap sleeves down my arms then let the dress fall in a pile at my ankles. He hoists me up and I wrap my legs around his waist, my hips starting to rock against him in need as we continue kissing. He slowly lowers me down onto the bed and pulls back so he can start discarding his own clothes. I watch with hooded eyes as he takes off his tuxedo coat, unwraps the tie and slowly starts to unbutton his shirt to reveal a rock-hard chest and abs. I lick my lips when his hands start to unbuckle his belt, then go to his button and zipper. Our breathing and the sound of the zipping being pulled down are the only sounds in the bedroom. He lets his pants fall to the ground and my eyes zero in on his bulging erection.

I sit up and I can't stop my hands from reaching out and pushing his underwear down his legs, his gigantic cock begging for attention. I lick my lips before wrapping my hands around his shaft, squeezing it slowly as I rub my thumb against his head. He inhales sharply while watching me guide him into my mouth. I close my lips around him and start licking up and down his cock, sucking gently on the tip. I repeat these actions until I firmly hold him with one hand and just concentrate on his head.

"Fuck, Ari, I'm not going to last long with that mouth of yours," He hisses as my mouth moves up and down his cock. He thrusts his hands through my hair and starts massaging my head while guiding it faster. I moan as I increase my pace and wrap my one arm around him, squeezing his ass while I suck him harder.

"Baby, I want to come inside you first," he rasps, and I slow my tempo down. With one last hard suck, I release him from my mouth and get on my knees to kiss him. He ravages my mouth before trailing hot kisses down my neck and clavicle, his fingers working to unhook the back of my bra. Once my breasts are free, he descends upon one of my nipples, making me moan out loud in pleasure. He continues his assault on my breasts, running his hands down my sides until he places his arm under my ass and scoops me up.

He gently lays me down, his hands grabbing the sides of my thong and bringing it down my legs and feet and tossing it to the floor. He starts kissing the insides of my thigh, my legs automatically parting wider for him. He moves up my legs and his tongue starts to lap up my clit, bringing me higher and higher to ecstasy.

"Please Warren," I beg him as I feel the tension starting to build. He stops sucking on my bud and inserts two fingers inside of me, pushing them in and out.

"Please what, baby?" he whispers while throwing my leg over his shoulder and I feel his lips starting to caress my clit again.

"I need you inside of me."

As soon as I say the words, he stands up, grabs a condom from the drawer in his nightstand and rolls it over his shaft. He takes the tip of his penis and brings it to my core, slowly rubbing his head up and down, teasing me until I reach up and grab his ass, trying to guide him inside of me.

"You're so fucking beautiful," he growls while slowly entering me, causing us to both moan out in desire. He starts rocking in and out of me, slowly at first but then his thrusts get harder, deeper. I watch him lick the pad of his thumb before bringing it to my clit and gently start to rub back and forth against it, matching the rhythm of his hips as he moves faster inside of me.

I bite my lip and moan, fisting the sheets on each of my sides. My walls begin to squeeze around him and I start panting as he thrusts faster and harder. I watch him throw his head back, about to roar out his release and the sight of how sexy he looks coming does me in. I scream out my orgasm, clutching his ass as I bring him harder against my pelvis, squeezing him tightly a couple more times until I go limp. He collapses on top of me and I wrap my arms and legs around him, keeping him locked against me.

I slowly come down from this euphoric high to feel his lips pressing kisses against my neck. He moves his forearms and pushes his weight up on them to look me in the eyes. His eyes shine with tenderness and lust and something else that my heart is hoping is love.

"My heart is yours, Ariana. No one else's. Are you ready to give me yours? Because there's no fucking way I'm ever letting you go."

Tears of joy spring to my eyes and I smile up at him, head over heels in love with this man. I cup my palm against his cheek and tell him the words that are coming straight from my heart. "It's yours, Warren. I'm yours."

Epilogue

ARI

Six Years Later

"LADIES AND GENTLEMEN, we're excited to welcome you today to the ribbon cutting ceremony for the brand new, state of the art Leighton Bentley Cancer Research Center. This center would not have happened if it wasn't for the determination, generosity and hard work of Warren Bentley and The Bentley Foundation. The city of Chicago is grateful to have another resource to help us find a cure for cancer. So please let's give a warm round of applause to Warren Bentley."

Warren plants a soft kiss on my lips before standing up and walking to the podium. He looks ridiculously handsome in his three-piece, navy-blue pinstripe suit and I shake my head in awe at how lucky I am to call that man mine. He shakes the mayor's hand and begins the speech that we wrote together on how this project was a dream of ours to leave a legacy behind for our mothers. I smile up at him in pride and love.

When he starts talking about our moms with their spirit and

strength to fight, tears spring to my eyes and I let one slip down my cheek before stabbing it away with my fingers. I feel my father, sitting next to me, grip my arm before patting it, his signal that everything's okay.

At the mention of her grandmother's name, our oldest daughter Kaylee looks up at me from her position on my lap and smiles sadly. She's wiser than her four years of age perceives her to be and it guts me that as she gets older, memories of her time with my mother will fade.

My mother lived for over three years after her first visit to the Blackburn Institute and within that time, so much happened to make her want to fight to stay alive. Warren proposed six months after the masquerade ball, and I officially turned in my resignation as his personal shopper one month before the wedding. Our wedding was a small, intimate affair with only our loved ones and close friends, exactly the way I wanted it to be. Warren took me on a three-month honeymoon around the world and to our surprise, I quickly became pregnant with our first child. We were excited to quickly become pregnant because it was important to me for my mother to meet her grandchild.

I went back to school to get a degree in nonprofit management, but declined the offer to become the director of the Bentley Foundation. Instead, I'm a board member and help guide the director on making our visions for the Bentley Foundation become a reality. I wanted to spend as much time as I could with my mom and be around for our children.

My mother cherished her time with Kaylee, but when we welcomed our son Asher two and a half years later, her energy levels weren't the same. It was clear that the cancer was overtaking her body and unfortunately, there was nothing else the Blackburn Institute could do to help sustain her any longer.

She didn't want to die in a hospital and per her request, Warren rented a house on Lake Michigan big enough for our whole family with a nurse to live in until her time was up. She died peacefully in her sleep.

To say I was devastated was an understatement. A piece of my heart is forever broken and if it wasn't for Warren, I would still be a mess. He's been my rock since the first moment he came barging into my life. He's erased all the financial burden that was on my family and has taken care of my father. I also think the timing of having Asher was kismet. I believe it was my mother's spirit giving me strength each day to get out of bed and be the best mother I could be in those early days after her death.

Warren finishes up his speech and motions for me to join him in cutting the ribbon. I hand Kaylee to my father and kiss Asher's cheek, who's sitting in his Aunt Delilah's lap. The city officials make room for me to stand next to my husband and I put my hand over his on the scissors as we cut away the ribbon. Warren literally took my dreams of wanting to find a cure for cancer and is trying to make it a reality. This project was his idea, a need for him to try to do our part in keeping our mother's spirits forever alive. I close my eyes and can feel my mother here with us today. When I open them back up again, I'm astounded at the love and support I can feel from our loved ones in attendance – my father, Delilah, Warren's grandmother, Olivia, Cal, and Jenna and so many other amazing people are here, cheering us on in happiness.

"Your mother is smiling down on you right now, so incredibly proud," I whisper in his ear as he hugs me tightly during the round of applause. He grabs my face and crushes his lips to mine, not caring who's watching or taking our photo. I throw my arms around his neck and put everything I am into our kiss.

"I love you forever, Mrs. Bentley," he whispers against my lips before moving them to my ear. "Now let's go home and make more babies."

Intrigued by Cal and Jenna Harrington's love story? You can read their second chance at love in Heartbreak Warfare, available on all platforms!
https://authorjessicamarin.com

Also By Jessica Marin

The Let Me In Series
Heartbreak Warfare (Let Me In, Book 1)
Perfectly Lonely (Let Me In, Book 2)
Edge of Desire (Let Me In, Book 3)

Bear Creek Rodeo
The Irish Cowboy
The Celtic Cowboy

Standalone Novels
Love At The Bluebird
(co-written with Aurora Rose Reynolds)
Until Valerie: Happily Ever Alpha World

Acknowledgments

Thank you to all of the readers and bloggers who take the time out of your day to read my work and support me. Your positive feedback and love mean the world to me.

Thank you to my family, especially my husband and children. Without their support, I wouldn't be able to continue living my dream.

It truly takes a village to make a book come to fruition and I couldn't have done it without the following people: All the wonderful ladies on my ARC Team, Najla Qamber, Tracey Vuolo, Barbara Hoover, Emina Ros, Crystal Reynolds, Christina Smith, and Brittany Holland.

Thank you to my Misfits for your continued love, support and promotion of all things Jessica Marin.

Please make sure you follow me on all of my social media pages and sign up for my newsletter at authorjessicamarin.com to be up to date with upcoming releases and book signings.

I look forward to our next adventure together!

Peace and love,

Jessica

About the Author

Jessica Marin began her love affair with books at a young age from the encouragement of her Grandma Shirley. She has always dreamed of being an author and finally made her dreams of writing happily ever after stories a reality. She currently resides in Tennessee with her husband, children and fur babies.

Jessica would love for you to join her on all of her available social media outlets. Do you love being a part of exclusive reading groups? Then join Jessica Marin's Misfits on Facebook!

Don't do social media? Join Jessica's newsletter to stay up to date with everything in Jessica Marin's world, including new releases, exclusive teasers and FREE BOOKS! You can sign up for Jessica's newsletter by visiting her website at https://authorjessicamarin.com